FUDGE DOINGS:

BEING

Tony Fudge's Record

OF THE SAME.

VOL. I.

Solomon Fudge

FUDGE DOINGS:

BEING

Tony Fudge's Record

OF THE SAME.

IN FORTY CHAPTERS.

By Ik. Marvel.

VOL. I.

NEW YORK:
Charles Scribner.
1855.

W. H. TINSON,
STEREOTYPER,
24 Beekman St., N. Y.

TAWS, RUSSELL & CO.,
PRINTERS,
No. 26 Beekman Street

LETTER OF DEDICATION.

TO

Dr B. Fordyce Barker,

Of New York.

My Dear Doctor,

When I began the papers which make up these volumes, I had no intention of giving them the form of a story; I purposed only a short series of sketches, in the course of which, I hoped to set forth some of the harms and hazards of living too fast—whether on the Avenue, or in Paris; and some of the advantages of an old-fashioned country rearing.

It seemed to me that there was an American disposition to trust in Counts and Coal-stocks, in genealogies and idle gentlemen, which might come to work harm; and which would safely bear the touch of a little good-natured raillery. By the advice of my publisher—who thinks, like most people now-a-days, that the old-fashioned race of essay readers, is nearly extinct—I worked into my papers the shadow of a plot, and have followed it up, in a somewhat shuffling manner, to the close.

The whole affair touches upon matters of money and of morals, which we have frequently talked over by your fireside, with a good deal of unanimity of opinion. I think you will agree with most of my sentiments, and only disapprove of the way in which I have set them down. Indeed, I wish as much as you, that the book had been better made, with more currency of incident, and more careful management of characters. But it has been written, you know, under a thousand interruptions; some chapters date from a country homestead, others from your own hospitable roof; still others have been thrown together in the intervals of travel through Italy, Switzerland, and France. I have seen no "proofs;" and have trusted very much (and very fortunately) to the kind corrections of my friend Mr. Clark, of the *Knickerbocker Magazine.* I know it is a pitiful thing for a writer to make excuses for his own neglect; and I do it now, less in the hope of gaining a hearing from the public, than of winning your private charity.

Such as the volumes are, however, I dedicate them to you.

Once more, I want to guard you against the error of thinking, from any tone of satire which may belong to the book, that the writer is wanting in regard for the worthiness of the good people who live around you. I claim, you know, to be an adopted son of your city; and it is a claim of which I am proud. I can never forget the kindnesses which have met me there; and whose recollection brings a pleasant home feeling to my heart, whenever I catch sight of Trinity spire lifting over the houses.

There seems to me a world-wide heartiness about New York, which promotes a larger hospitality for opinions, and for people, than belongs to any other American city that I know. New Yorkers wear their hearts—like their purses—wide open. They may fall into errors: but they are true American errors of a generous liberality. It is in keeping with the spirit of our institutions to use large trust towards all men: New Yorkers may lose by it, in their purses, as they sometimes do in their homes. But the loss, even, seems to me worthier than the gain, which is secured by a close-eyed suspicion, and a prudent inhospitality.

I am glad that you are now fairly domesti cated in that Prince of American cities. I know that you will find your way in it to fame, and to fortune: and I hope that you will wear always your old cheerfulness of look, however rare may prove the epidemics.

Truly Yours,

DONALD G. MITCHELL.

PARIS, 20TH OCTOBER, 1854.

CONTENTS.

Fudge Doings.

INTRODUCTION.

"First, my fear; then, my courtesy; last, my speech."
DANCER'S EPILOGUE.

I MUST confess that I feel diffident in entering upon the work which I have taken in hand. Very few know what it is to assume the position that I now occupy; viz., endeavoring to entertain the public with a record of the observations, fancies, history, and feelings of one's own family. Many people do this in a quiet way; but I am not aware that it has heretofore been undertaken in the unblushing manner which I propose to myself.

I shall expect misrepresentation and calumny. It will not surprise me to find some squeamish individual of the Fudge family denying my claim to membership, and roundly asserting that I am not the Tony Fudge I profess to be. I am prepared for such denial.

I shall expect the Widow Fudge to refuse all sanction of my papers as veritable history, and to declare stoutly that the writer is an impostor ; and that such incidents as I may set down, in my simplicity, are utterly without foundation, and entirely unknown to herself, as well as to every respectable member of the Fudge family. I shall expect the Miss Fudges to turn up their noses at many little expressions of moral doctrine which will come into my record, and to sneer publicly at my portraits of their habits and tastes. I shall, without doubt, be disputed by them on the score of age, clearness of complexion, accomplishments, and such other matters as may make good the pictures of my excellent second cousins, the Miss Fudges. For this, I am prepared.

I shall furthermore expect that Mrs. Phœbe Fudge will utterly deny my statements with respect to her weight. I doubt even if she will admit the truth of what I shall have to say regarding her public charities, and her interest in the Society for the Relief of Respectable Indigent Females. She will very possibly deny the truth of any comparisons

I may draw between her expenses at Lawson's, and her droppings into the poor-box of Dr. Muddleton's church. The chances are large in favor of her repudiation of all relationship with any man who calls himself TONY FUDGE; and of the additional assertion, that such individual can never have seen good society, and must therefore be thoroughly ignorant of whatever concerns herself. Indeed, I am prepared for it.

Mr. Solomon Fudge, her husband, who is another estimable member of the Fudge family, I shall expect to trouble himself very little about my remarks, so long as I confine myself to his wife's foibles, her virtues, or her boudoir; these are matters which concern him very little; but when I touch upon the gentleman's financial engagements, or upon some recent suspension, when moneyed rates "ruled high" (whereby some few small friends subsided into insolvency), I shall anticipate a certain fidgety manner, and an abrupt refusal of all kinship with his very excellent nephew, TONY. I am prepared for this.

It would seem that I was undertaking a very odious employ, in thus provoking the wanton assaults of so many members of my own family. But I shall be consoled with the reflection, that I am doing no inconsiderable service to the public, as well as elevating the Fudge family into a certain historic dignity.

There are few people, after all, who will not risk a great deal of their modesty, and a very respectable fraction of their morals, for the sake of a prominent position in the public eye ; and however much my dear cousins, and kin of all sorts, who come under the Fudge arms, may rail at my indiscretion, and my lack of breeding, they will, I venture to say, hug the *éclat* which my rambling record will give to their character and name.

With this much of preface, which I contend is more to the purpose than most of the prefaces of the day, I shall enter at once upon my design.

I.

BEING HISTORICAL AND PERSONAL.

> "THE poor Americans are under blame,
> Like them of old that from *Tel-melah* came,
> Conjectured once to be of *Israel's* seed,
> But no *record* appeared to prove the deed;
> Thus, like *Habajah's* sons, they were put by
> For having lost their *genealogy*."
>
> REV. COTTON MATHER.

THE Fudge family is large. Where it originated, I cannot well say. Many lady members of the family are of opinion that it is very old, and can be traced back to some of the bravest of those Norman knights who did battle against Harold. They have adopted the crest of some of those heroes in support of this belief, and wear the same upon their fingers. I can hardly conceive of a prettier argument, or one more prettily handled. Reverence for antiquity is a delightful trait of the female character. A romantic admiration for knights and men-at-arms is a charming characteristic of the sex.

It would be unwise to discredit openly a lady's statement in respect to her paternity, or to make light of any argument by which she supports the dignity of her family. My own opinion is, however, that it is much more probable that the Fudge family would find its true origin in the more humble antiquity dating with the Restoration. This limit would throw out at once all Puritanic taint, which I observe it is becoming quite fashionable to discard, and would furthermore be strengthened by a host of probabilities, in view of the great increase of family names which grew up under the pleasant auspices of Charles the Second and his court.

I would by no means impugn the motives of those members of the family who wish to go farther back, or question the taste of such crests as they have adopted. The Miss Fudges, my excellent cousins, Bridget and Jemima by name, are particularly tenacious on this point; their tenacity, moreover, is well sustained by the use of signets, and a very creditable air of *hauteur*.

I am sorry to say that I cannot learn that our family was ever much distinguished; and I have been shocked to find the name of Fudge among the humblest purveyors for King Charles's camp, before the battle of Worcester. This, however, is proof of a strong royalist feeling, which still obtains to a very considerable degree among the lady members of the family, particularly one or two interesting spinsters, who divided a season, two years ago, between Homberg and Wiesbaden.

Upon the Newgate Calendar I find, on close inspection, only two entries of the name. I regard this as a very flattering circumstance.

The first is that of Johnny Fudge, who, in the reign of Queen Anne, was convicted of horse-stealing at a June term of the York Assizes, and was condemned (III. Ph. and M. c. 12) to the gallows. The second appears to have been a criminal of much more character and consideration. It appears that in the first half of the reign of George III. one Solomon Fudge was indicted for seditious and treasonable acts. What the precise nature of the acts were, does not appear upon the calendar; I cannot doubt that they were worthy of the reputation of the family. We learn, that after a royal reprieve, Solomon was a second time the victim of the law, and expiated his offences, in the year of grace 1760, upon Tower Hill.

Miss Bridget Fudge, indeed, who is of kin with the present Mr. Solomon Fudge, and who has latterly worked a very brilliant ancestral tree in pink and yellow *chenil*, on silk canvas, insists that the name of these culprits was spelt Foodge; and that they could not therefore have been connected, even remotely, with Jacques de Fudge, *Baron de La Bien Aimée*, who lost a spur or two at the battle of Hastings. It certainly is an open question, well worthy of a doubt, if not of discussion, at the hands of the Historical Society.

For my own taste, I would much prefer to leave ancestral inquiries in the dark; and feel confident that if the same trepidation and fear of issues belonged to most of our ancestral inquirers about town, they would wear much safer names, and infinitely better repute. Hap-hazard will do very much more for the most of them, than Heraldry; and I have a strong suspicion that, in slighting the claims of Hap-hazard, they are slighting the claims of a veritable progenitor.

As for the history of the Fudges, since they have become a portion of the American stock, little can be said which would not apply with equal pertinency to nearly all the first families of the country. A stray scion has now and then, in a fit of love, demeaned himself by intermarriage with the daughter of some plain person; or, in an equally unfortunate fit of policy, brought about by habits of extravagance, he has sought to supply the "needful" by obtaining possession of some heiress of the town, who had little to recommend her, save a passable grace in the dance, and a moderately taking eye.

By these unfortunate casualties, it has happened that the purity of the original Fudge stock has become singularly impaired. It is even hinted, among the knowing gossips of the family, that the late Solomon Fudge, father to the present Solomon Fudge, made a sad slip in this way, and contracted an awkward-looking, left-handed marriage, very much to the exasperation of all the spinster connections of the family.

It appears that the old gentleman was rather frisky in his young days, and after a certain *affaire du cœur*, which threatened to create great scandal in the family, he was fain to marry his mother's waiting-maid. She, however, proved a most notable house-wife, and provoked all her married kin-folk with a swarm of the liveliest and ruddiest children that had been known in the Fudge family for several generations.

More attention, however, is now given to the race. I have already alluded to the ancestral tree worked in *chenil*, and to the crests. The spinster members of the family particularly, have shown great caution; they are waiting for "blood."

Indeed, I may say, they have already waited for no inconsiderable time.

Although the stock may be made nobler under this regimen, I have my doubts whether it will be made any purer or stronger. I have therefore recommended to my cousin Bridget, who is not indisposed to change her condition—seeing that she is now verging upon her thirty-fifth year—a comely man in the retail line, who lives nearly opposite her house in the town, and who has shown repeated attentions through the medium of a small-sized ivory-mounted opera-glass.

I should hardly venture to urge the matter, unless I knew that the gentleman alluded to is about retiring upon a competency; and with a slight change of name, a suit of black in place of gaiters and plaids,—to break up any old associations which might prove unpleasant—I really think that he would prove a most eligible partner for Miss Bridget. Of course, she affects, as most young ladies do, proper disdain for any one recommended by a gentleman-friend; but I understand that she is by no means careful to avoid his opera-glass observation. This is certainly a rather promising sign.

Miss Jemima, her sister, is prim and wiry, and takes to books. I shall have more to say of her as I get on.

As for myself, I have lived off and on, about the town, for some twenty-odd years. Naturally, I verge upon middle age. Very few, however, I flatter myself, would suspect as much. I am particular about my wig, waistcoat, and boots. My wig has a careless, easy effect; my waistcoat is never unbuttoned and never stained with my dinner; my boots always fit. I am thoroughly convinced that proper attention to these three points is essential. They diffuse the charm of youth and grace over the bodies of individuals otherwise mature.

I am married—only to the world; which I find to be an agreeable spouse, something fat, and with streaks of ill-temper; but, upon the whole, as good-natured and yielding as a moderate man ought to expect.

I think I might easily pass for a man of five-and-thirty; I have been mistaken for a younger man even than this. I profess to be a judge of chowders, sherries, and wines generally. Sometimes I dine at the club; sometimes with a friend; sometimes with my esteemed uncle, Solomon Fudge; and on odd afternoons, with the widow Fudge, Miss Jemima, and Miss Bridget Fudge.

I admire beauty, and have had, like most men, my tender passages.

At eighteen, I was in love with a widow of thirty-five—madly in love. My opinion is, that if she had not left the country unexpectedly, I should have died at her feet, or at her fire! At twenty-one, I was engaged to a blonde of three-and-twenty, with very blue eyes, and of a demure countenance, which I still remember with considerable sentiment. It was broken off with mutual good-will, and with some heart-burnings on both sides. She has now five children, lives in Thompson street, and weighs, I should guess, near upon two hundred: her husband puts it at a figure or two less. I call her Mabel, and she calls me Tony.

At twenty-four I was desperate. I am of opinion than no man was ever more so. Sir Charles Grandison, in comparison, was a tame lover. The scarlet waistcoat, that I wore at that particular epoch, seemed of a dingy ash color. I not unfrequently put it on, through absence, with the back-side in front. I lived entirely upon vegetables. I wrote a surprising number of sonnets. I think the number of lines in each was altogether unprecedented.

But, alas for human hopes!—she proved a coquette. I forgave her after two weeks, during which I suffered intensely, and forgot her in four. It is my opinion that she forgot me about the same time. Now, however, she is a cheerful spinster. I sometimes take a dish of tea with her. I observe that she begins to use hair-dye.

Since that time, I have been variously enamored of married and single women ; the latter generally quite young. The very last could hardly have been more than sixteen. My opinion is, that I am more attractive to individuals of that age, than to older girls. They are certainly more attractive to me. The absurd fallacy that young men are more successful lovers than the middle-aged, is now quite clear to me. I begin to appreciate the good judgment of the sex. Ladies are by no means so silly as young men take them to be. I am quite confident that my power of fascination was never so great as since I entered upon my fortieth year. I do not affirm that the same could be said of all bachelors of similar age.

I have undertaken to be personal in this chapter, and shall not therefore spare my modesty. It is not my way to halve things : if my story is to be told at all, it shall be fully told.

As for my more immediate family history, however, I do not propose to enter into particulars. Like most men about town, I am at present my own master, and trust that nothing will interrupt this private mastership for some time. I rely very little upon any Fudge counsel, and am not much in the habit of boasting of my Fudge ancestry.

My opinion is, that in this country a man must stand upon his own feet, and not upon the decayed feet of any family ancestors. It is pleasant to be a member of one of the first families, such as the Fudges undoubtedly are, and, if assertion can retain the place, will unquestionably continue to be.

Individuality seems to me the best stamp and seal that a man can carry: if he cannot carry that, it will take a great deal to carry him. If a man's own heart and energy are not equal to the making of his fortune, he will find, I think, a very poor resort in what Sir Tommy Overbury calls "the potato fields of his ancestors;" meaning, by that cheerful figure, that all there is good about the matter is below ground.

I shall stand then simply upon my merits and my name: and if my cousins Bridget and Jemima question my hardihood, my only reply will be—Fudge!

In case the reply should not prove satisfactory, and the hungry critics should belabor me, after their usual fashion, as a man of no calibre and of but little dignity, I shall still sustain my first-mentioned position, and meet all their cavils with a single reply; and that reply will be—Fudge!

II.

My Uncle Solomon.

"Statio in *Dignitatibus*, res lubrica est."
VERULAM: SERM. FID. XI.

MR. SOLOMON FUDGE is not a man to be sneered at. His friends all know it; and he knows it better than his friends. I have referred to him already. At present, I mean to draw his portrait. He will be flattered, doubtless; this is natural in nephews and in artists.

He will feel flattered also; yet I have no doubt that he will meet me in a very indignant manner, and say to me, with a great show of dignity—perhaps adjusting his shirt-collar meantime—"Tony, you should have known better than this; you should have considered, sir, our family position. Mrs. Fudge, sir, your aunt (before referred to as a stout woman), is a lady of delicacy; great delicacy, I may say."

I expect this, and am prepared for it. I shall reply :

"Uncle Solomon, you know you are glad to be noticed : you know that you possess a cheerful fondness for distinction. You are not to be blamed. No man is : you are worthy of it."

Whereupon my uncle Solomon will take off his gold spectacles, pass them from one hand to the other, in an eccentric yet methodical manner, which is a way he has of collecting his thoughts.

"Tony," he will continue, "I beg you will be discreet. Ridicule, sir, I shall not bear, even from a Fudge."

To which I shall reply, in a kind way :

"Uncle Solomon—FUDGE !"

I now proceed with my portrait.

Mr. Solomon Fudge is a stout man, with white hair. He usually wears a white cravat ; a clean one every morning, as he has himself told me, and an extra one when he invites a friend to dine with him. He is a merchant, and lives in the Avenue ; he has also a country-seat at Astoria. If he were to die—I hope he will not—he would be mentioned by the Wall street journals (for the first time) as an eminent merchant ; liberal, distinguished, and leaving a large family, inconsolable.

He began life as errand-boy in a large jobbing

establishment: he swept out the store at sunrise; he has often told me of it; not very often, however, of late years. I am of the opinion that it is only latterly that he has begun to form proper notions about family dignity.

At the time of his being alderman for the first time, he seemed proud of his rise in the world. He is now above being alderman. He looks upon aldermen generally as moderate men. He has once been mayor; he now regards even mayors as mere city contingencies. Still, however, he often refers to the year when he was in authority; a remarkable year he thinks it was, for clean streets and good order. Most retired mayors, I observe, hold the same opinion in regard to the period of their mayorship.

Mr. Solomon Fudge, is a bank-officer in Wall-street. You may see him on discount-days, luxuriating in a stuffed chair and easy posture. One arm will very likely be stretched out upon the table; the other will fall carelessly upon the elbow of his chair. He appears to enjoy the sunshine. His gold-bowed spectacles will be raised upon the upper part of his forehead, and rest with great apparent security over that portion of the brain where phrenologists usually locate the bump of benevolence. As I remarked, the bump does not interfere with my uncle's spectacles.

His words are slow and measured, as becomes a man of his grave aspect and undoubted family. He is cautious in his expression of opinion ; and only ventures upon decided approval of "accommodation paper" when he is very sure of his man, or when the applicant's wife has been in a position to show favors to Mr. Solomon Fudge's wife. Uneasy and anxious-looking men, full of business, and in need of loans, he regards with a very proper degree of distaste.

Few visitors can call my Uncle Solomon from his chair, or—what is a still stronger mark of deference—occasion the withdrawal of the gold-bowed spectacles from the secure position already hinted at. If I were to except any, it would be a certain dashing broker, of whom Mr. Fudge has a trifling fear, or some grey-headed curmudgeon who is a federal officer, or some visiting English merchant ; or, yet again, some old lawyer of reputation.

The newspapers he reads with a kindly and patronizing interest, having little respect, however, for anything smaller than the huge folios of Wall street. All young men and new men in the province of journalism, are very properly treated with contempt. He makes an exception in favor of one of the small morning newspapers, which is distinguished for its advocacy of the tariff. He hopes it may "eventuate" (that is his style of language) in something practical. The truth is, my uncle Solomon has no inconsiderable interest in a manufacturing establishment in the country, which is just now running at half-time, and with very small show of profits. If he could sell at a fair figure, I think he would subscribe, without solicitude, to the tenets of the *Journal of Commerce.*

He is usually a cautious man, and rarely makes a false step. Just now, indeed, he is feeling a little sore in respect of a large purchase of the Dauphin stock. The affair, however, came so well recommended, with such distinguished patronage, and the sample-coal burned with such a cheerful flame, that he thought it little worth his while to examine into the nature of the veins, or the probability of very frequent and surprising "faults." The consequence is, he is down for some fifteen thousand present valuation, which I greatly fear may stand him in some two-score.

My uncle Solomon is a vestry-man; and though not a church member, he has a most respectable opinion of the whole scheme of religion: he believes it ought to be supported; he means to do it. He pays a high price for his pew; he invites the clergyman to dine with him; he foregoes his extra bottle of wine on such days; he feels a better man for it;

he humors nis wife in a fat subscription to the indigent orphan asylum; he subscribes for the *Churchman;* he sometimes reads it. He is the proprietor of one of the most magnificent Bibles upon the Avenue, to say nothing of a set of prayer-books, with solid gold clasps, guaranteed as such by Mr. Appleton the senior, and corroborated by actual inspection of Ball, Tompkins, and Black.

His charities, notwithstanding what I have hinted about the spectacles and the organ of benevolence, are upon that large scale which is such a favorite with the established gentlemen of the town. By established gentlemen, I refer to such as have a great reputation for respectability, wealth, white cravats, dignity, composure, and good taste in wives and wines. By the large scale of charities, I refer to those mission societies which publish yearly lists of distinguished donors to public dinners, aid to political enterprises, Union committees, and purchase of ten per cent. bonds of western railways (secured by mortgage on timber lands), which are represented to be in a needy condition, and worthy objects of eastern charity.

Indigent men about town—I do not here refer to myself—and poor cousins, do not stir to any considerable degree Mr. Solomon Fudge's benevolence. He has good reason to show why. He thinks every man should take care of himself. What is true of men is true of women. He thinks there is great reason to apprehend imposture. He has known repeated instances of the grossest imposture. He fears that the poor do not go to church. He thinks men should be cautious. He *is* cautious—saving the Dauphin speculation.

Upon the whole, Mr. Solomon Fudge is what people call an estimable man. Jemima and Bridget both regard him with considerable awe. Street-folk generally look up to him. There is not a man in the whole city—and on this point I challenge investigation—who is treated with more deference by his coachman and his grocer.

I have myself considerable esteem for my uncle. He is a portly man, calculated to impress. He does not dress shabbily, saving rather too much dandruff on his coat-collar. I have recommended a wash: he slighted it. His wines are good, with the exception of the last lot, purchased "at a bargain" from the Messrs. Leeds. He has a few boxes left of some mild old Havanas, the gift of a tenant, who begged a month's deferment of quarter-day, and ran off in the interval. Mr. Solomon Fudge has a small opinion of the cigars: *I* insist that they are good.

Mrs. Fudge, the wife of my uncle Solomon, and naturally my aunt—by marriage—I entertain a cheerful regard for. I am of opinion that she entertains much the same feeling for me. Neither her person nor character can be digested hastily. She will fill a chapter.

III.

Description of Mrs. Solomon Fudge.

——"tam suavia dicam facinora, ut male
Sit ei qui talibus non delectetur."

Scip. from Mr. Burton.

MRS. FUDGE is of the family of Bodgers, of Newtown. It is by no means a low family. Her father was Squire Bodgers, a deserving, stout man, rather bluff in his habit of speech, but "fore-handed," and quite a column in the Baptist Church of Newtown. Indeed, the only serious quarrel which ever occurred between my Aunt Phœbe and the Squire, was in relation to church-matters. Mrs. Fudge, after ten years' residence in town, ventured to change her faith—simultaneously wlth her change of residence from Wooster street to the Avenue. From having been an exemplary Baptist, she became, on a sudden, an unexceptional high-church listener, with prayer-books and velvets to match.

Mr. Bodgers, of Newtown, was indignant, and came to the city on a visit of expostulation. My Aunt Phœbe tried reasoning, but the Squire was too strong for her. She next tried tears, but tears were unavailing. She urged the wishes and the position of her husband, Mr. Fudge ; to all which I have no doubt that Mr. Bodgers replied, in his bluff way, "Fudge be d——d !" I do not, however, affirm it.

The result may be easily anticipated. Mrs. Fudge continued firm in her new connection ; reading the service at first with a good deal of snappish zeal, and at length subsiding into an eligible pew and place, where her furs would meet with observation, and her complexion catch a becoming light from the transept window. Mr. Bodgers threatened to cut her off from all share in his country estate ; and, to give color to the threat, brought about a reconciliation with his second daughter, Kitty, who had married, eight years before, very much against his wishes, a poor country clergyman.

How and where the courtship first came about which ultimately metamorphosed the plump and comely Phœbe Bodgers into the exemplary Mrs. Solomon Fudge, it seems hardly worth while to narrate. It is sufficient to say, that the wife of Squire Bodgers was a shrewd woman and capital manager. Solomon Fudge was a disinterested young man, of eligible family, pleasant prospects in the way of trade. He wore, judging from an old portrait which ornamented the back-parlor in Wooster street, and which hangs in the basement upon the Avenue, the tight pantaloons which were in vogue at that date, and a considerable weight of metal to his fob-chain.

Numerous incidents in regard to the courtship have leaked out, from time to time, when I have found my aunt in a sentimental humor ; but as they appear to be mostly of that ordinary and common-place character which are found in novels, and have little of the spice of real life about them, I do not think it worth my while to write them down. A little sonnet, however, in acrostic form, in which Phœbe Bodgers figures as Diana, has gratified me as an evidence of considerable poetic taste on the part of the present bank-officer ; and I need hardly say, that the same is carefully guarded by Mrs. Solomon Fudge.

Squire Bodgers, I regret to say, is now dead ; so is his wife. Mrs. Fudge, though fat and healthy, is an orphan. She cherishes, I regret farther to say, but a slight recollection of the surviving members of the family. The old gentleman, in dying, was as good as his word, and left but little of his small property to the town-branch. The homestead reverted to Mrs. Kitty Fleming, the widow of the poor clergyman already mentioned, who died, leaving one child, bearing the mother's name and a fair share of country beauty. I have met with her on a random visit to Newtown in the summer season. She is just turned of sixteen. I am not aware that she speaks a word of French ; yet I must confess that I admire her exceedingly—much more than her aunt.

Mrs. Solomon Fudge does not fancy Newtown as a summer residence ; she rarely alludes to the place ; nor does she often speak of her country cousins. They paid her frequent visits while she was living in Wooster street ; I observe that they have since fallen off. When they come, however, she is familiar and easy with them—in the basement. I do not remember that she ever gave a party for them.

One stout, fussy old gentleman, who has been a thriving shop-keeper in her native township, annoys her excessively. Upon the strength of a very remote cousinship, he insists upon addressing her as "Cousin Phœbe ;" and this notwithstanding he wears a long surtout and a prodigious red-and-yellow silk pocket-handkerchief. His name is Bodgers—Truman Bodgers, Esquire. He has been in the State Legislature, and did a great deal for the tanning-interest of the county, in which he is himself largely interested.

From some hints that have been now and then dropped, I incline to the opinion that Mrs. Fudge was an old flame of his : it is certain that he keeps up a moderate show of attention to this day. He is one of those genuine, rough-bred country Americans who are not to be pricked through with any stings of fashionable observance. He counts his Cousin Phœbe no better in her home upon the Avenue than when she played bare-footed at the old husking-frolics of Newtown. And with a straightforward native instinct, he acts out his impressions in plain country fashion.

I must say that I rather admire Mr. Bodgers, notwithstanding my aunt's ungracious sneers ; and I admire him all the more for the wholesome contrast that he offers to my poor aunt's city weaknesses. Next to her dread of his coming, I think that she manifests a decided reluctance to my meeting with him at her house. The consequence is, as I am an amiable man and have much spare time on my hands, I almost always contrive to call whenever I catch a glimpse of the long surtout ; and enjoy exceedingly the rubicund countenance of friend Truman, and the slightly vinegared aspect of Mrs. Solomon Fudge.

I think I have dwelt long enough upon the antecedents of Mrs. Fudge ; I shall therefore go on to speak of her present home, character, and position.

She is an exemplary woman ; at least, this is the style in which her clergyman, the Reverend Doctor Muddleton, uniformly speaks of her. I observe, however, that he speaks in the same way of a great many others among his lady parishioners, who rent very high-priced pews, and subscribe in a fair sum to his pet charities. It is, upon the whole, a discreet way of speaking. Dr. Muddleton is a discreet man.

My aunt, then, is an exemplary woman : what the Doctor means by it, I could never precisely understand. She is certainly an example of apparent good health, and of fair preservation ; in point of size, too, as I have already remarked, she is quite noticeable. She does not believe in unnecessary fatigue of any sort. The world wags very quietly with her, and she sees no reason why it should not wag very quietly with everybody else.

She is methodical and judicious in her charities: she suffers her name to appear in the public prints—although a great trial to her natural delicacy—as one of the managers of the Society for the Relief of Indigent Females: she makes a small yearly contribution to the same. She gives her maids several old silk dresses in the course of the year, and supplies her cook with cast-off under-clothes. She presents her coachman every Christmas-day with a half-eagle; and on one occasion, when he wished "A 'appy New-Year, and many of 'em, to the hiligant Mrs. Fudge," she extended her charity to a cast-off over-coat of her husband's.

She does not allow match-girls, and that sort of vulgar people, to be begging about the basement windows. She rather prides herself upon the dignified and peremptory way with which she orders them off; it certainly is not apt to provoke a return.

Her house is after the usual city pattern—two parlors, with folding-doors; one furnished with blue, the other with crimson. Two arm-chairs to each, of rosewood, very luxuriously upholstered. Straight-backed chairs, with crewel-worked bottoms and backs; one or two of these. A screen similarly worked, one of Peyser's best. Ottoman, similarly worked; a red-and-white puppy, in crewel. Alabaster vases, from Leeds' auction, "quite recherché in form," as Mr. Leeds remarked at the time of sale. Candelabras, of fashionable pattern, from

Woram and Haughwout—"a splendid article." Tapestry carpets, very soft, arabesque pattern, quite showy, and, according to the Messrs. Tinson, "remarkably chaste." Curtains, to match furniture, very heavy cord and tassel, draped under the eye of Mrs. Fudge, by a middle-aged man, of "great taste."

There are paintings on the wall, very strongly admired by Mr. Bodgers, and country cousins generally. They were imported at immense expense, but purchased by Mrs. Fudge at a bargain. A dining-room skirts the two parlors in the rear. This arrangement of the house is not original with Mrs. Fudge; several city houses are built in a somewhat similar manner. I do not know that this arrangement suits Mrs. Fudge's convenience and family better than any other; I do not think, indeed, that she ever asked herself the question. It is the style; and my aunt has a great abhorrence of anything that is not "the style."

Mrs. Fudge has at her command a coachman and footman. The first sticks to the stable; the second does duty in-doors—cleans the silver, waits on the table, and receives visitors. On ordinary days he wears a white apron; but on great occasions he is ornamented with a blue coat and Berlin gloves. Mrs. Fudge supplies him with soap and shaving materials. She ventured at one time, after reading Cecil, into powdering his hair. Mr. Bodgers mistook him for Mr. Fudge. I came near falling into the same mistake myself. She has abandoned the powder.

If I were to call Mrs. Fudge a fashionable lady, I should do violence to her prejudices, at the same time that I should gratify her affectionate impulses. I have not so much fear of her violence as I have love for her gratification. I therefore say unhesitatingly, Mrs. Fudge *is* a fashionable woman.

"Tony," she will say, "you know better. You know that I scorn fashion; you have heard me do it again and again. You know I have a perfect contempt for all the extravagances of fashion."

"Quite as you say, Mrs. Fudge," I should reply, blandly.

"Why then do you call me fashionable, Tony?" (quite mildly, and with a felicitous tweak of her cap-strings, followed by a careless yet effective adjustment of the folds of a very showy brocade dress).

"I was doubtless wrong, Aunt Phœbe. It was a mistake of mine. You are not a fashionable woman."

The face of Mrs. Fudge falls. She thanks me very sourly, and she insists upon knowing what conceivable reason should have suggested such an idea.

In an ugly humor—we will say after one of the cold breakfasts of the down-town hotels—I should reply, "None at all;" thereby gratifying my aunt's moral sentiment, and making her my enemy for ten days to come. I know better than this; a man does not live for twenty years about town for nothing. My reply would be, therefore, very different. "Reasons enough, Mrs. Fudge. You employ a fashionable hair-dresser; you trade only at fashionable shops; you wear the most becoming and fashionable colors (imagine Aunt Phœbe's glow); you drive at a fashionable hour; your furniture is fashionable; and the names in your card-basket are fashionable names."

This last assertion (the only really questionable one of the whole) she admits as strong evidence against her. But how on earth can she refuse the visits of such persons as *will* come?

"How, to be sure?"

Mrs. Fudge is all smiles. She will not listen to my talk of leaving. She will speak of me (I know she will) all the week as that dear, delightful fellow, Tony.

There is a large swarm of persons upon the town —heads of families and others—who without being fashionable themselves, are very earnest but very silent admirers of what they think fashionable society. They are, I observe also, very indefatigable in their raillery of fashionable follies, and in their expressions of contempt. They follow after the camp with very much show of mirth, and with a great deal of eagerness to catch up a cast-away feather or a cockade. They rail at what is out of their reach, and have not the apology of refinement to give a zest to their cravings.

Having whipped my chapter upon Mrs. Fudge into this smack of a moral, I shall close it here.

IV.

Wishes, Ways, and Means.

"Into the land of trouble and anguish, from whence come the old and young *lion*, they will carry their riches upon the shoulders of young asses, to a people that shall not profit them."—Isaiah xxx: 6.

I HAVE a fear that many will have already misconceived Mrs. Fudge's character: they will set her down in their own minds as a vain, careless woman, with no definite purpose in life.

Mrs. Fudge has a purpose. Ever since she ceased to be a Bodgers, and began to be a Fudge, she has cherished this purpose. Ever since she left Newtown for a life in the city; ever since she eschewed the Baptist persuasion for the refinements of Dr. Muddleton's service; ever since she pestered her husband into a remove from Wooster street to the Avenue, a gigantic purpose has been glowing within her. That purpose has been to erect herself and family into such a position as would provoke notice and secure admiration. There may be worthier purposes, ·but there are few commoner ones. Mrs. Fudge is to be commended for the pertinacity with which she has guarded this purpose, and measurably for her success.

Wealth Mrs. Fudge has always religiously considered as one of the first elements of progress: she is not alone in this; she can hardly be said to be wrong. Mr. Solomon Fudge is a rich man. I could hardly have adduced a better proof of it, than by my statement of the fact that he is a large holder of the Dauphin stock. None but a substantially rich man could afford to hold large stock, either in the Dauphin or the Parker Vein Coal Companies. Such humble corporations as pay dividends (which they earn) are generally held by those poor fellows who need dividends. Mr. Fudge needs no dividends. Coal companies generally pay no dividends.

Mrs. Fudge, for a considerable period of years, has made the most of her wealth. She is, however, a shrewd woman; Uncle Solomon is a prudent man; she has, therefore, made no extraordinary display. She has kept a close eye upon equipages, hats, cloaks, habits, churches, different schemes of faith and of summer recreation. She is "well posted" in regard to all these matters.

Unfortunately—I say it with a modest regret—a certain Bodger twang belonged to my aunt, which the prettiest velvet cloak, or the most killing of Miss Lawson's bonnets, could never hide. *I* regard it as a native beauty, redolent of the fields; *she*—I am sorry to affirm it—does not regard it at all. It has, however, I am convinced, stood in the way of her advancement.

For five years she may be said to have occupied the same position; the seasons hardly counted upon her; they were certainly not counted by her. She enjoyed a certain prestige of wealth; as much, at any rate, as could be forced into laces and withdrawn readily from the stock-broker's capital. Her children held ignoble positions, either in the nursery or at school. At one time, indeed—I think it was during the cholera-season—she came near ruining her prospects in life by gaining the reputation of a domestic woman. She has since, however, very successfully counteracted this opinion.

I have spoken of the children of Mrs. Fudge. Children are an ornament to society; greater ornaments, frequently, than their parents. With a city education, and with the companionships that grow up in a city school, they possess a foot-hold, as it were, which could never have belonged to Phœbe Bodgers. Mrs. Fudge understands this; she has had an eye to this matter, in the course of her son's schooling: her daughter she has watched over with the same motherly care.

Respectable little girls have not unfrequently been invited home to tea by Wilhelmina Ernestina, at the instance of the mamma of Wilhelmina Ernestina. The same little girls, of good family, have been invited out to ride with the mamma of Wilhelmina Ernestina. The mamma has taken great pleasure in talking with such little girls; and has kindly amused them by instituting comparisons of her furniture, or her dress, or her tea-service, with the furniture, and dress, and tea-service with which the little girls of good family are familiar at home. From all this, Mrs. Fudge has derived some very valuable hints.

In short, Wilhelmina Ernestina is a perfect treasure to Mrs. Fudge. Her point-lace pantalets attracted considerable attention while they were still living in an obscure mansion of Wooster street. Wilhelmina has, moreover, a passably pretty face. It has a slight dash of bravado, which, considering the uses to which it is to be applied, is by no means undesirable. She is just now upon the point of "coming out;" and, as much depends upon her action and success at this particular period, her mother and myself naturally regard her movements with a good deal of anxiety. I shall take pleasure in recording, from time to time, in the course of these papers, her perils and her triumphs.

Her son, George Washington, more familiarly known to the family as Wash. Fudge, is a promising young man. He is an ornament to the street: he is immensely admired by two very young girls over the way, much to their mother's mortification.

I shall venture to draw a short sketch of his appearance and habits: the sketch will not, however, be a *unique.* Several portraits of him already exist; Mrs. Fudge herself possesses two in oil and three in Daguerreotype. He has, moreover, bestowed several upon young ladies about town, to say nothing of a certain Mademoiselle who became enamored of him—to use his own story—and who holds a highly respectable position in the choir of a distinguished opera troupe.

Wash. Fudge has had some twenty years' experience of life—mostly town-life. He is, therefore, no chicken. This is a favorite expression of his, and of his admirers. He dresses in quite elegant style. I doubt somewhat, if such waistcoats and pantaloons as ornament Wash. Fudge can be seen on any other individual.

He was entered at Columbia College : there was not a faster man in his class. His mother advised association with such young gentlemen as appeared to her—from the catalogue—to be desirable companions. She even contrived a few oyster-suppers in the basement, to which they were invited. The affair, however, did not succeed. The young gentlemen alluded to did not return the civilities of young Fudge. Miss Wilhelmina Ernestina, although set off in her best dress, and playing some of her richest bits of piano practice, did not seem to do execution on a single one of the young gentlemen above alluded to.

Wash. Fudge decided Columbia College to be a bore ; he determined to leave the faculty. The determination was happy and mutual.

He now devoted himself to dancing, billiards, and flat cigars. His progress was very creditable. Mrs. Fudge took a great deal of very proper pride in the jaunty and dashing appearance of her son Washington. She had a not doubt of his growing capacity to do great execution upon the lady-members of New York society : he had already, indeed, given quiet proofs of his power in this way by certain dashing flirtations in small country-places. A trip to Paris was naturally regarded by Mrs. Fudge as a great opportunity for perfecting himself in the designs which he had in view. A trip to Paris was therefore determined on, somewhat to the demurral of Mr. Solomon Fudge, but much to the satisfaction of his son and heir.

Mrs. Fudge flattered herself that the Miss Spindles, and Pinkertons, and other young females of distinguished families, would find him perfectly irresistible on his return. She saw herself the envied mother of one of the most delightful young men about town—to say nothing of the accomplished and fascinating Wilhelmina Ernestina. She saw, furthermore, her advances upon the fashion of the town sustained by the unremitting attentions of young gentlemen of distinction, and by such overflowing receptions as would for ever bury all recollection of the Bodger blood.

I wish calmly to ask if Mrs. Solomon Fudge is to be blamed for all this? Are not great numbers of mothers anxious and hopeful in the very same way? Nay, do they not continue anxious and hopeful from year to year, trusting in Providence, money, and management, to secure their ultimate rescue from the shades of second-rate society? Is it not reasonable to expect that six years of coaching, at the very pick of the hours; adroit charities to well-known city institutions ; persistent listening to the Rev. Dr. Muddleton ; positive familiarity with Miss Lawson, will in time, effect their purpose; and that the stout Mrs. Solomon Fudge will, supported on the wings of Wilhelmina and George Washington, soar to the utmost height of society and of ton?

V.

WASH. FUDGE ABROAD.

"YEA, I protest, it is no salt desire
Of seeing countries, shifting a religion,
Nor any disaffection to the state
Where I was bred (and unto which I owe
My dearest plots), hath brought me out: much less
That idle, antique, stale, grey-headed project,
Of knowing men's minds and manners, with ULYSSES:
But a peculiar humor of my *mother's*."

VOLPONE: BEN JONSON.

THE speech of Mr. Politic-would-be, in Ben Jonson's play, twangs as admirably with the humor and intent of Wash. Fudge, as he set off upon his travels, as can be imagined. Mrs. Fudge and Wilhelmina waved their handkerchiefs theatrically from the Jersey dock, as the steamer which bore George Washington paddled off into the bay. Mr. Solomon Fudge waved his hat, in the graceful manner which he had learned when returning the plaudits paid to him as Mayor of the city.

I cannot say that the parties were much overcome, on either side. Mrs. Fudge, as usual, bore up stoutly. Wilhelmina might, I think, have shed a tear or two, had her eye not lighted, in the very moment of her enthusiasm, upon a dashing fellow upon the quarter-deck : and she conceived the sudden and cruel design of fascinating him where he stood.

I have no doubt that the basilisk eyes of Wilhelmina were fastened upon the gentleman above-named, at the very moment that she twirled her handkerchief for the last time, toward the dimly-receding figure of Wash. Fudge, and subsided gracefully into the arms of her mother. Her position was a good one upon the dock. Mrs. Fudge had arranged her dress as she supported her ; the cambric handkerchief, which waved adieu, was trimmed with lace ; the wind was moderate ; the by-standers were numerous ; and the whole affair was creditable.

As the crowd dispersed, Miss Wilhelmina recovered her spirits and her footing.

As for Wash. Fudge, who had learned some experience in the nautical line, by one or two excursions in mild weather, in a small sloop-rigged yacht, to Coney Island, he avowed himself to various parties on ship-board to be quite in his element. The element seemed to be kindred with his qualities down the bay, and for some twenty hours thereafter. After this, it would appear that young Mr. Fudge was less talkative than usual: he seemed fatigued; he reposed frequently upon the settees lashed to the "lights" of the after-cabin. His appetite failed him, especially at breakfast. There were very violent calls for the steward from state-room number fourteen, such as could hardly have been anticipated from a dashing yacht-man, in his own element.

I am told that there is something excessively awkward in the position of a ship's decks at sea. My opinion is that Wash. Fudge experienced this awkwardness very sensibly. I can imagine my young friend, wedged of a morning very tightly in the angle formed by a thin mattress and the wall of his state-room, the victim of irresolution, and of considerable nausea. I can fancy his plaid pantaloons swinging over him, in a very extraordinary manner, from the farther side of his room, the contents of his wash-bowl plunging toward him very threateningly, and the bedclothes, and ship generally, wearing a very bad smell. In any delirious attempts to dress, I can easily imagine him making sad plunges toward the leg of his pantaloons, sometimes taking a rest, with his hand in the wash-bowl, and struggling frightfully to recover the escaping end of his cravat. Under these circumstances, and while recovering some composure by a resort to a horizontal position, I can imagine the contrast afforded by the pleasant, off-hand manner of the English steward, as he announces breakfast: and I think I can picture to myself the parched and yellow expression of my usually cheerful young friend, as he listens to the appetizing and kind enumeration of "Grilled fowl, Sir! nice curry, Sir! broiled bacon, Sir!"

Young Mr. Fudge has been specially commended by Mr. Fudge, senior, to the Captain. The Captain would not, of course, fail to be obedient to the wishes of Mr. Fudge, late Mayor, etc. He pays them the same degree of regard which sea-captains usually pay to such demands upon their time and attention. On the third day, perhaps, he pays a visit to his *protégé*:

"Eh, bless me! not out yet, Mr. Fudge?—rather under the weather?"

Master Fudge replies faintly: not at all in the manner of a yacht-man.

"Ah, well, brave it out my man: eat hearty: stir about: rather nasty weather, this. Good morning."

A bottle of old particular Madeira, secured upon the first day, holds its place obstinately in the rack: Mr. Fudge finds that taste changes at sea. A nice little pacquet of flat cigars, on which he had counted for a vast deal of luxury, are entirely discarded. The same may be said of a nicely-ruled diary, in which Mr. Solomon Fudge had suggested the record of such practical observations as occurred to his son upon the voyage. There are, indeed, a few notes upon New-York bay: brief mention of the first day's longitude, and one or two observations upon steam-engines. In a letter to an old companion, eked out upon the calm days, Wash. Fudge shows himself more discursive, and possessed of more fertile resources:

"Dear Tom," he writes, "hope you are well and thriving down at Bassford's to-night: can't say the same for myself. The motion is different from that of the Sylph, and the engines keep up an infernal clatter: prefer sailing, myself. Beside, one has no appetite: the truth is, I've been a little under the weather. My chum, a chubby Englishman, in grey coat and gaiters, shaves regularly at eight. I expect to see him cut his throat every breezy morning: it would be a great relief.

"I don't know as you were ever sea-sick; it's uncommonly annoying!

"I have managed a game or two of piquet, with a nice, gentlemanly fellow aboard; but he plays devilish well: no very tall figures; but I'm in for three or four pound. I mean to learn the game.

"There's a confounded pretty girl aboard—Jenkins is her name—with her father or uncle, I don't know which. I wish you'd find out who they are, what set, etc., and let me know. She's deuced stylish. No chance for flirtation aboard ship. When you come, Tom, don't, for Heaven's sake, count on any great dash. It's no go. The style is a stout sou'-wester, and grey pants: only at dinner a little show of waistcoat and fob-chain.

"I take pen again to tell you the voyage is up. Irish shores in sight. Uncommon low, black steamers they have this side. Am in for four pound more at that infernal piquet: mean to learn it. Give my love to the boys."

From the Adelphi, Liverpool, Wash. Fudge, in obedience to maternal wishes, communicates such facts as he trusts will be interesting to Mrs. Fudge. I quote only a few passages, which certainly show a condensed and pointed style, as well as careful observation:

"Immensely stormy passage and there were great fears of being lost: at which I hope you will not be alarmed, as it is now over. Was sick for a day or so, but soon over it. There was a pretty Miss Jenkins: blue eyes, uncommon pretty hair. Do you know any family of that name? Write me if you do: also anything else interesting.

"Liverpool is quite a large place, but foggy, very. The ladies hold up their clothes at the crossings considerably higher than in New-York: clogs pretty general. Don't dress so prettily: rather taller than they are at home: fatter, too. Haven't seen many fine faces: Miss Jenkins's is the prettiest.

"They gamble badly on board ships. It is melancholy to think of it. Kept a diary, but it's too big to send with this, postage being high. Shall write again from Paris or London, can't now say which.

"Love to Wilhe. Yrs. aff'y."

At London, Wash. Fudge is quartered at Morley's Hotel; and in obedience to the reiterated wishes of Mr. Solomon Fudge, he transmits to that gentleman a brief record of his observations. I beg to premise, that Mr. Solomon Fudge, with true business tact, had always recommended great precision of language, no redundancy of words, and close observation of foreign habit, especially in all that related to commercial life, into which line he has a strong hope of one day warping his son's somewhat scattered habits.

"My dear father," writes Washington, "for account of voyage please see mother's letter of 6th: also for general notes on Liverpool. The docks are large, of brown stone, containing an immense deal of shipping. They are called Prince's dock, Salt-house dock, Queen's dock, and others: all said to have been dug out of the cemetery, which seems probable, as the cemetery is very deep.

"Delivered Mr. M.'s letter the 4th. Counting-rooms in Liverpool are dark, in other respects resemble those of New York. Dined with Mr. M. next day: expressed regard for you. Dinner much the same as at home, only sit longer over wine: glass of porter served. Beef is specially tender and juicy. Waiter wears white gloves, ditto cravat. I think this description of a British merchant's dinner will be agreeable to you.

"Left Liverpool Monday. They call the cars carriages: stuffed seats, but very expensive. I am afraid, dear father, you will have to extend my credit two hundred pounds. Didn't see much of the country: should say it was fertile, very. Couldn't tell how many passengers there were, but rather a long train.

"As you have seen London, I will not describe it. A young gentleman came on with me, who has kindly showed me a good many of the buildings, theatres, and others: but as he is rather a gay lark, I think I shall avoid him some.

"I go to church on Sundays: quite a large church at Liverpool, with a chime of bells. I have not been to the docks yet, but hope to, in case I leave by sea. I shall go to Paris shortly, and remain, meantime, very dutifully, etc."

Not being myself very familiar with London, I do not wish to be considered personally responsible for any statements above made. It is, perhaps, needless to remark that Wash. Fudge visited the Tower, the Hay-market, and London Bridge, with great apparent interest; he was also particularly struck with the huge sentry at the gate of the Horse-Guards. In short, like most young Americans, Mr. Fudge turned his back upon England, with only such knowledge of British habit as could be picked up along Oxford street and the Strand, and with such acquaintance with the British country and agriculture as may be gained in the Park of St. James, or in the "Long Walk" of Windsor.

At Paris, Wash. Fudge is again, as he expresses

it, in his own element, notwithstanding a very unfortunate ignorance of the language. He takes rooms, as most fresh Americans do, upon the Rue Rivoli, and commences observations of continental habit by minute study of the long-legged English, and dashing couriers, who usually throng the court-yard of Meurice. These observations, being of a valuable character, he jots down for Mr. Sol. Fudge, of Wall street, in this strain :

——"Thus far it appears to me that the French are a tall people, and talk considerable English : some wear gilt bands on their hats. They (the bankers) have their offices in their houses, and call them, very funnily, *bureaux.*

"Paris is an expensive place, and I hope you will remember about the credit : am glad to see Dauphin is rising : hope it will keep rising. M. Hottinguer was very polite : asked me to step in occasionally, and read the papers. They call the Exchange, *Bourse*, I find, and do considerable business. It is a building with pillars : theatre opposite. I rarely go to the theatre. They have beautiful gardens here : Tuileries, and Mabille, and others. Occasionally they dance in them. The French are fond of dancing. I shall probably practise a little.

"As you advised me to pay attention to business matters, called to-day at several shops on the Rue de la Paix. The shop-keepers are very polite. A great deal of wine is sold in Paris. Some newspapers are published. I have not had much time to read them. The form of government is republican. People seem contented, especially at the balls up the Champs Elysées (translated, means Elysian Fields). Am getting on pretty well with French. A good deal of order seems to prevail. The wine is made in the provinces. I have not yet seen the provinces: am told they are very extensive: also the vineyards. Have not yet seen the President, but a good many cuts of him: the cuts are said to be very fair."

It may be as well to leave our cousin Wash. at this point, premising only that Mrs. Fudge, with true maternal regard, has cautioned her son against forming such associations abroad as would retard his advancement upon a return to New York, especially among American travellers. There was a time, indeed, when the rarity and expense of foreign travel was a certain guaranty for gentility; but now-a-days, as Mrs. Fudge very justly observes, the popular taste for European society and observation renders a great deal of caution imperative.

VI.

Other Fudges.

"Like to a double cherry, seeming parted,
But yet a union in partition.
Two lovely berries moulded on one stem:
So, with two seeming bodies, but one heart;
Two of the first, like coats in heraldry,
Due but to one, and crowned with one crest."

Shakspeare.

I HAVE already spoken of Mrs. Fudge, the widow, and of her daughters, Jemima and Bridget Fudge. I now take the liberty of introducing them more particularly. I feel sure they will appreciate the honor. They admire literary people. They adore sonnets. And if the two Misses Fudge were not rather old girls, there would be no safety for stray unmarried poets. They would be carried by storm ; particularly by Miss Jemima.

To Miss Bridget, as I have already observed, I have recommended a cheerful, retired, retail man, of an opposite lodging. The affair, however, does not progress beyond the opera-glass already mentioned.

They live humbly, in a street little known. Their parlors are dingy, but furnished in *recherché* style. There is a plaster cast, full length, of Juno ; another of Hebe ; attractive figures, both of them. There is very much crewel-work, for which cousin Bridget is famous.

Asking my readers up stairs, I beg to present them to the Misses Fudge, in their chamber. The thought of this will spread blushes upon their cheeks. They are seated by the window, commanding a view of the grocer's window, already alluded to.

Bridget is busy with her embroidery, relieved by occasional somewhat frigid glances over the way; where, presently, the identical grocer and opera-glass do, singularly enough, make their appearance. Jemima wonders that her sister can give any countenance to such awkward attentions. To which Bridget insists very strongly that such a thought had never entered her head; that she would not show enough notice of the gentleman to leave the window ; wonders her sister could have imagined such a thing; breaks her crewel in her mortification; hunts over her basket for the right color; pricks her finger, and relieves herself by an indignant look at her sister, and another furtive glance ever the way.

Jemima, meantime, having disposed a stray curl, which "gives" (as the French say) upon the street in a killing manner, rests her brow upon her forefinger (the ring is a row of pearls), and continues her reading of Tupper on Love.

The grocer improves the occasion to convey his hand to his mouth, and to waft what may possibly be a kiss across the way. Miss Bridget is, of course, horribly scandalized, blushes very deeply, glances at Jemima, lights up with a ray of sisterly affection, and without one thought of meeting opposite gallantries, conveys her hand innocently to her mouth, for the sake of drawing her crewel a little farther through the eye of her needle.

Jemima, meantime, sighing over some exquisite passage of Martin Farquhar, slightly changes the position of her fore-finger, so as to smooth the hair at its parting, employing the opportunity for a very virtuous glance over the way. The poor grocer, was just then unfortunately returning in a vehement way what he considered the advances of Miss Bridget. Jemima is very naturally shocked in her turn, and vents her excess of indignation upon Miss Bridget.

The quarrel would undoubtedly have ended—as such sisterly quarrels usually do—in tears, if at that very moment the maid had not made her appearance with a letter for the Misses Fudge.

I know nothing, so far as my own limited experience of the society of maiden ladies extends, which so sets in motion the blood of a prudish damsel upon the wrong side of the marrying age, whether it be twenty, twenty-five, or thirty (for these things are regulated more by character than by age), than the announcement of a letter. Whether it is that the frail residuary hope seems to lie in that imaginary form, or what may be the reason, I will not undertake to say. It is a singular fact.

The letter here in question was addressed in a manly hand—a strange hand; but, unfortunately, to the sisters in common. It could, therefore, contain no express proposal. Much as the sisters were attached to each other, I cannot but think that this indefinite mode of address was a source of regret to both.

Bridget had no doubt of its being from the gentleman opposite, who had availed himself of this ruse to open communication with herself. Jemima doubted as little that it was a waif of praise from some admirer of her poems, who was desirous of a personal interview.

After a pleasant sisterly quarrel, it was agreed that Jemima, being the more literary of the two, should have the opening of the mysterious paper, while Bridget should keep an eye over her shoulder, to see that all went off properly.

"My dear cousins!"

The surprise of such commencement compelled instant reference to the close of the letter.

"Pshaw!" said Jemima.

"Faugh!" exclaimed Bridget.

The name at the close of the letter was none other than that of Truman Bodgers.

The letter did not contain the slightest hint of any elopement; nothing of the kind. It was a business letter, yet arranged with tact and affection. I shall give the burden of it in my own way.

I have already spoken of Kitty Fleming, living in the same town with Truman Bodgers, and niece of Mrs. Solomon Fudge. I have expressed some admiration for the young lady named. It is needless, therefore, to remark upon her attractions: she is pretty. Mr. Bodgers knows it, and partly out of real kindness—for he is a man of the old stamp—and partly out of spite at cousin Phœbe, who has discountenanced his views, he is desirous of giving to Kitty a sight of the world, and a little "top-dressing," as he calls it, of city life.

With this intent he makes appeal to Misses Bridget and Jemima, thinking, I dare say, and with a great deal of discretion, that Miss Kitty will be eminently safe under their guardianship. Mr. Bodgers is a shrewd man, and, fancying that opposition to the plan would come chiefly from the "girls," has addressed the daughters rather than the mother: thinking, very plausibly, that if he could but open their hearts, the old lady, in virtue of a postscript relating to "compensation"—"feeling of delicacy"—"his own lack of family"—"no hesitation, etc.," would cheerfully comply.

"It's very odd!" said Miss Bridget.

"Very," said Jemima.

"Can he think of marrying her, Minny?"

"Nonsense, Bridget: he's forty."

"Forty's not *very* old, Minny, dear."

"I wonder if she's pretty?" said Jemima.

"They say she is: quite pretty, for a country-girl," said Bridget, despondingly.

Jemima's face lengthened in the slightest perceptible degree.

"How can we take her, Bridget dear?" said she.

"To be sure, how *can* we?" said Bridget, glancing over the way.

"Possibly she may be a belle," said Jemima.

"Who knows?" said Bridget, with an air of resignation.

"That would mortify Aunt Solomon," said Jemima, reviving.

"And Wilhelmina," said Bridget, cheerfully.

"Bridget, dear, I think she had better come."

The last view of the matter was decisive. The pretty Kitty Fleming is to be transferred from the qniet shades of Newtown to the small front chamber of the Widow Fudge.

Thus, upon one side we have the cheerful Wash. Fudge in plaid tights, coquetting with the heroines of the Mabille, while the elegant Miss Jenkins looks on coldly from the distance.

Upon the other, we have the timid Kitty, making her entrée upon New York life, supported by the affectionate sisters, Jemima and Bridget, while the dashing Wilhelmina appears in the back-ground, covering gracefully the retreat of Mrs. Solomon Fudge.

VII.

Kitty Leaves Home.

"It is sweet to feel by what fine-spun threads our affections are drawn together."

Sterne.

THE proposal of Mr. Bodgers in reference to our friend Kitty had been naturally the subject of very much and serious reflection. Mrs. Fleming, it will be remembered, is a lone woman: Kitty is her only child. Not only this, but the mother, like most country ladies after the flower of their life is gone by, had a secret dread of the city. It is a natural dread, and is well founded.

If I had myself been consulted, I should, notwithstanding the gratification of meeting with my pretty country cousin, have shown considerable diffidence of opinion. There is a bloom, I have observed, indigenous to country-girls, which is almost certain to wear off after a year's contact with the town. This bloom, I am aware, is not much valued or admired by city ladies generally; they cultivating, in its stead, a certain *savoir faire*, as they term it; which, being translated, means, very nearly—a knowledge of all sorts of deviltry.

Mr. Bodgers is a well-meaning man, and his regard for his young *protégée* would not have been surprising, even in a married man; much less is it surprising in a bachelor. I do not mean to hint that he entertains anything more than a fatherly feeling for Miss Kitty. On this point I am not capable of judging. The tendencies of gentlemen over fifty in this regard, are exceedingly difficult of analysis. I have met with those of that age who fancied themselves as provoking, in the eyes of young ladies, of the tender passion, as they ever were in their life. If this be true, they must, in my opinion, have passed a very uninteresting and unprofitable youth.

The spinsters of Newtown are divided in opinion as to the attentions of Mr. Bodgers: the elder portion insisting that his matrimonial inclinations (if he have any) tend toward the mother; and the younger portion insisting, with a good deal of sourness in their looks, that the "old fool" is in love with Miss Kitty herself. Such busy and uncomfortable talkers are not uncommon to country-towns.

What Mrs. Fleming's views may have been, I will not undertake to say ; she was certainly most grateful for the kindness of Mr. Bodgers ; and, had it not been for her widowed state, might possibly have entertained the thought that he had serious intentions with respect to her daughter.

I say it is possible ; for I have observed that mothers generally do not make the same nice distinction between a man of fifty and a man of twenty that girls are apt to do. Indeed, I flatter myself that they are disposed to look with more favor upon the man of the latter age, well established in life, than upon youngsters of two or three-and-twenty. It is seriously to be hoped that the coming generation will be educated in the same substantial and creditable opinions. In that event, single men may look forward to a very brisk and long-continued nomad state of bachelorship, which, when fairly exhausted, will yield them a blooming partner, with whom to idle down those flowery walks of a virtuous old age, which end in a gout, a crutch, and the grave-yard.

Kitty Fleming has not been nurtured in these opinions. She has never counted the attentions of Mr. Bodgers in any other light than as the kind offices of an affectionate and whimsical old uncle. Yet even Kitty herself has had misgivings in regard to her acceptance of this last kind offer.

It is strange how early a sense of propriety grows upon some minds, and how, by their very nature, some souls will shrink from what, to the common mind, seems only an honorable advantage. Kitty, with those soft, yet keen blue eyes, has not been blind to the tattle of the gossips of her little village; and there is a shrinking from whatever will incur and provoke their remark. And added to all this, is the dread of leaving the places and the friends she has always loved.

The city multitude knows little of that fond attachment to place, which grows up under the shadow of ancestral trees, and which spreads out upon the meadows that have seen all the youthful gambols and joys of the spring of life. Brick-houses and First-of-May movings cannot foster the feeling, which twines its heart-tendrils among the mosses of old walls, and around ivy-covered trellises: and there is nothing in a street-name, or in a number, that so clings to the soul as the murmur of a brook we love, and the shadow of a tree whose leaves we have made preachers of holiness and of joy!

And yet Kitty, woman-like, has her vague long-

4*

ing for a sight and a sense of that great city which is every day whirling its multitudes through the mazes of gain and of pleasure. Alas, for our human weakness! Who is bold enough, and who is pure enough, at whatever age he may be, not to lust after the "pride of life?"

But against this craving, which belongs to our little Kitty (to whom did it ever not belong?) come up again the home attachments; not all confined to that old mansion, which has so long borne up the very respectable name of Bodgers. Indeed, those attachments are very wide-spread.

I do not at all mean to say that little Kitty was at this particular time the victim of any very tender passion; I should be very sorry to think it. Nor do I mean to say that she imagined herself such victim; she would certainly never allow it. And yet it is quite surprising how actual parting does discover a great many little meandering off-shoots of affection, whose extent, or presence even, we had never before imagined. Nothing but positive removal will expose the multiplied fibrous tendrils by which a plant clings to its natal place; and sadly enough, it often happens in the same way, that our lesser affections never come fairly into view, with their whole bigness, until they are broken.

There never was a country-girl, I fancy, verging on seventeen, with eyes one-half so bright as Kitty's, or a complexion one-half so tell-tale, or with such fine net-work of veins to braid their blue tissues on the temple, without counting up divers, of what the French call, *affaires du cœur*. And these matters are recorded, for the most part, by withered nosegays, silk-netted purses, embroidered slippers, and moonlight walks. If there be any one devoid of such experiences, she must be very much colder-blooded than my little coz Kitty.

At least such is my opinion; an opinion corroborated, I do not doubt, by Mr. Harry Flint, one time student, and now attorney, of Newtown. The name is, or was, familiar to Kitty. I have seen her blush at the bare mention of it; which fact she will strenuously deny.

The heart of seventeen is, however, a very uncertain, capricious heart. Its loves are, for the most part, sentimental impulses. It has no fair knowledge of its own strength. So it was, that though Kitty had sometime felt a little tremor at a touch of Harry's hand, and had looked with rather approving eyes upon a certain honest and ruddy face which he was in the habit of wearing, and had accepted his protection, on certain occasions, against such lurking assassins as are apt to prowl about village walks of an evening; and although, all things considered, she preferred him to the majority of people—out of her own family—she had never fancied there was any special depth, or indeed measurable capacity of any sort, about her feeling; and was half frightened to find how big a space he filled in the blank of separation.

As for Harry Flint, it would be wise for him to keep by his law, and forget as soon as possible a country-girl on the eve of a city life. She will be very apt to forget him. I would advise him to put the embroidered slippers, which he now cherishes like two objects of vertu, to daily and secular use. And as for the pressed flowers in his Bible (which he is shy of lending), it would be well to transfer them to his herbarium, if they possess botanical value, and not to trust to any other value whatever.

A boy at twenty has no more right to be in love than so young a girl as my little coz. Nothing more than sentiment belongs to that age: between which and affection there lies a vast difference. There are plenty of people without the latter in any bulk, who class them both together. Such people are proper subjects of pity. Sentiment is febrile and impulsive. Affection is continuous and progressive. Hurt sentiment shocks prodigiously; but hurt affection cuts like a sword-blade.

The sentiment that dwelt in Kitty bound her to many things, and many people—Harry Flint among the rest. Affection dwelt more at home: and it glowed very deeply as she lingered there (I know how it must have been) upon the bosom of her dearest friend, struggling to say, what she could not say with a firm lip—"Good-by, mother."

I can imagine even my friend Mr. Bodgers in his long surtout, putting his yellow silk handkerchief once or twice to his eyes, under the foul pretence of blowing his nose, and saying very briskly, "Pogh, pogh!" Nay, he has tried to hum a short tune, and walked to the window to observe the weather, without, however, making any observation at all. He has positively taken up a book from the parlor-table, and seems for a moment interested in it, notwithstanding he holds it upside down.

At a little lull, however, Mr. Bodgers gains courage, and begs Kitty to "cheer up," and be a "brave girl," and fumbles his cornelian watch-key in a very impatient manner.

Still Kitty lingers, and the mother clasps her tightly.

A six months' or a year's parting between mother and daughter is surely no great affair: and yet a lurking, vague presentiment of change, accident, alienation, will sometimes make it full of meaning. Besides, the mother was alone; Kitty the only mortal to love; life was full of change. And with Kitty, too, the great city she had hoped to see, dwindles now; so small, so insignificant is the world of Form, when measured by the world of Affection! With this feeling rushing on her suddenly, and with one of those swift soul-measurements of time and life which the over-wrought heart will sometimes call up, she forgets her little scheme of pleasure, and she will stay in her own home; she will not quit it—ever!

"Bless me," says Mr. Bodgers, "Kitty, child—Mrs. Fleming, dear me—Kit—pshaw—psh"—— Mr. Bodgers is taken with a slight turn of coughing, which we would hardly have looked for in a man of such perfect health.

It is curious how a mother's resolution will grow with necessity; and just now it spread a calmness over the mother's action that availed more than all the "pshawing" and "bless mes" that Truman Bodgers ever uttered.

And Mrs. Fleming spoke very firmly, all the more firmly because so very gently.

"Kitty, my dear, you will go: I wish it. You will enjoy it, Kitty; you will improve, I am sure. Then you will write me, Kitty, very often; and you will see your cousins, and will come and see us again in the summer. Kiss me good-by, Kitty."

"Good-by, mother," falteringly.

And Mr. Bodgers buttoned his long surtout, and gathered up his umbrella; and with Kitty clinging to his arm, and looking back, they left her home together.

And there were village girls outside, to say, "Good-by, Kitty;" and there were old servants and poor women, who had felt her kindness, to say, "God bless you, Kitty!" And there were boys who took off their caps, with a kind of cheerful mourning, to bow a farewell; and others, older and less cheerful, to wave a hat sorrowfully, and after that a handkerchief persistently, and with a slow, saddened action, that must have taught Kitty that a great many people loved her.

And the trees braided fantastic shadows along the old village walks, where recollection went walking yet. And the hills stooped kindly to the blue sky, in silent, sad greeting; and the belting woods far away, east and west, trailed autumn wreaths of gay colors along either side the road, by which Kitty went away from her village home.

It may be that Mr. Bodgers thought regretfully of what joys had been cast from him, and lost for ever, as he watched the sad, earnest face of his little *protégée,* lingering yet with her eye upon the vanishing town. It may be that the hope of some warmer feeling overtook him, as he felt her impassioned grasp of his arm, as she clung to him, while her thought wandered before her into the strange scenes they were approaching.

As for Harry Flint, working at his tasks, it would be hard to say what thoughts came over him when he knew that she who had lighted up a good many fairy dreams of his was gone, where a thousand objects would arrest her regard; and where the modest country-girl would become such mistress of the forms and fashions of the city, as would blunt all the force of his homely and honest affection.

It would be very absurd in him to think any farther of the city belle; of course it would. He will doubtless forget her in six months; of course he will.

Mr. Bodgers (Harry Flint would give all his patrimony to be in his place), sitting very trimly in his long surtout beside Kitty, meditates pleasantly upon the prospect of that admiration which he knows must belong to his little *protégée.* There never was an old country-gentleman, with a pretty kinswoman, who did not feel perfectly satisfied that such kinswoman would be excessively admired in the city, and become, as it were by necessity, one of the reigning divinities. Such old gentlemen are, it is true, frequently mistaken; New-York being a large place, and there being an incredible number of well-looking women distributed over it, of almost every age and condition.

As for Kitty, her thoughts ranged very widely; sometimes floating over the new scenes and new companions, and again jumping back, by a kind of electric action, to the old and cherished friends she had left behind. In evidence of the last, Kitty did now and then, notwithstanding the homely encouragement of Mr. Bodgers, drop a low sigh.

"None of that; pray don't, Kitty. They'll treat you well. They are pleasant old girls."

This sounded to Kitty disrespectful.

"They'il give you a storm of kisses; they don't often have a chance of that kind."

Mr. Bodgers chuckled slightly at his own shrewdness.

"And, Kitty" (Mr. Bodgers spoke in a fatherly manner), "be careful of your heart."

Kitty looked archly at him.

"Plenty of butterflies will be flitting about you. Take care of them; they've no brains."

Kitty looked disappointed.

"They carry all they're worth upon their backs."

Kitty looked surprised.

"And, by the by, Kitty, where's your little purse?"

"Full, sir; ten dollars in it at least," very promptly.

Mr. Bodgers smiled; but whether at Kitty's *naïveté*, or at thought of doing a good deed, I do not know.

"Hand it to me, Kitty."

And Kitty drew out a very thin *porte-monnaie*, with certain letters scratched upon it, which she kept out of sight.

Mr. Bodgers thrust in a small roll of bills.

"Uncle Truman!" said Kitty, but in such an eager, kind way as tempted him to search in his pocket for another roll.

"Be prudent, Kitty; and let me know when it's gone."

Kitty hesitated, with her eyes glistening in a most bewitching way.

"No nonsense, Kitty; I am an old fellow, you know. I've no use for money—no wife, you know;" and there was a dash of tender regret in this.

Kitty took the purse, and laying it down in her

lap, placed her little hand in the stout hand of Mr. Bodgers.

"You are *so* good to me, Uncle Truman!"

"Nonsense, Kitty!" and Mr. Bodgers coughed again, very much as he had coughed in the little parlor of Newtown.

The wind was fresh, and perhaps he had taken cold.

VIII.

How the Fudges Worship.

"A very heathen in her carnal part,
Yet still a sad, good Christian at the heart." Pope.

I BEG to return to Mrs. Solomon Fudge. She is in her pew, within the brilliant church of the esteemed Dr. Muddleton. The parti-colored light plays very happily: the pink reflection upon herself, the blue upon Wilhelmina, and a dark shadow upon the scanty-haired pate of Solomon Fudge, late mayor, bank-director, and vestryman.

The church is, as I said, a brilliant one, and by virtue of the coloring within and without, creates the illusion of a gigantic hot-bed, in which the velvets, plumes, and gauzes figure as chrysanthemums, orange-flowers, and azalias; and the Reverend Doctor, in his modest *soutane*, accomplishes the gardener—who applies the steam, and who, with rare nicety of judgment, secures such an even and gentle atmosphere as quickens the vital succulence, and promotes to an enormous extent all floral develop ment. The Doctor, however, does not pluck his flowers—save only in a spiritual sense.

The Doctor has advanced some distance in his discourse, but Mrs. Fudge is not, I regret to say, over-attentive to its burden; on the contrary, she is thinking intently of Geo. Wash. Fudge, and of the Jenkinses. I will not say that proper thoughts have been wholly out of her mind. She has meditated upon the pleasing intonations of the Doctor; has indulged in agreeable speculations upon the quiet and repose of the church-services. Nay, she has pitied Miss Scroggins, who has a seat behind the column; has indulged in a compassionate regard for the Miss Slingsbys, who have uncommonly sharp noses, and for Mrs. Scrubbs, whose daughter has made a run-away match with a poor man.

Mrs. Fudge has gone even farther: she has determined to give her blue watered silk (having seen one precisely similar upon the person of old Mrs. Gosling) to her waiting-maid. She has made her responses in a reverent tone; she has mused with half-closed eyes upon the nicety of Faith and Religion; she has experienced a cheerful glow in her spirits, and feels proud and happy that a comfortable doctrine can diffuse such charity and contentment over her somewhat ambitious life. The old-fashioned Baptist ministrations were sometimes annoying: Dr. Muddleton, dear, good man, is never annoying. She wonders if he is engaged to dine on Thursday; and if he likes a *filet—à la sauce piquante*, or served plain?

From all this, however, as the Doctor progresses, her reflections warp, as I have said, to a consideration of Geo. Wash. Fudge, now in Paris, and of the Jenkinses. She wonders who the Jenkinses are? She has asked several friends. Her friends do not know the Jenkinses. Still, it is quite possible that the Jenkinses are—somebody.

She figures to herself Geo. Washington, the husband of a rich and elegant Miss Jenkins—living in style—giving small, *recherchés* dinner-parties—sprinkled with foreign guests—spoken of in the Sunday papers—highly fashionable. She portrays to herself Miss Jenkins in very glowing colors. She murmurs to herself, "Mrs. Geo. Washington Jenkins—Fudge."

She pictures to herself her dear Wash. in plaid tights, with an eye-glass, and Paris hat, and short stick set off with an opera-dancer's leg, and a large budget of charms, brilliant waistcoat, and moustache. She fancies him quite the envy of all the stylish mammas about town; half the stylish young ladies dying for love of him. She fancies him very carelessly winning some literary consideration—writing sonnets as if they were beneath him—patronizing poor "penny-a-liners," or possibly himself the suspected author of a poem in the *Literary World.*

Then there is Wilhelmina Ernestina. Mrs. Fudge has reason to be grateful to Providence for such a daughter. She is showy. Mrs. Fudge, with matronly solicitude, has 'put her through' an unexceptionable course of French phrases and pantalets. Wilhelmina is positively beginning to startle attention. There were certainly fears for a time; but Wilhelmina *is*, as I said, become an object of remark. Her hat alone would insure it. Miss Lawson, in that hat, has outdone herself; and, strange as it may seem, has outdone her usual prices. Miss Lawson—for a wonder—has exerted herself.

Wilhelmina has not a bad face: not indeed so tell-tale, or so wrought over with blue veins, as her cousin Kitty's; but it is even better adapted to the work on hand. It is a striking face; her eyes are not tender, but good-colored, and well cultivated. Her figure is firm, tall, and jaunty; her hand not over-small, but reduced considerably by Chancerelle's gloving.

It is my opinion that Mrs. Fudge bears her daughter considerable affection, especially in Sunday trim. It is my opinion that Wilhelmina bears her mother considerable affection, especially in view of the tempting baits which Mrs. Fudge holds out to fashionable young men.

It would be interesting to notice the proud glances which Mrs. Fudge, in the intervals of Sunday reflection, throws upon Wilhelmina's hat, or her glove, or the exceedingly pretty fit of her basque waist. Mrs. Fudge only regrets that more eyes do not see it than her own. She fairly pines at the thought that such charms should not be doing execution upon the susceptible and highly advantageous young Spindle—son of the wealthy Spindle. Wilhelmina, by request, appears entirely unaware of her mother's enraptured glances.

I have said that Wilhelmina had admirers. They are not, however, very acceptable to Mrs. Fudge. Mrs. Fudge is ambitious—very. So is Wilhelmina.

Mrs. Fudge has not spent her life, and money, and affection (wasted upon Solomon) for nothing. Wilhelmina is not to be thrown away—not she. An old clerk of her father's—a sensible young man in other respects—has sent repeated bouquets to Wilhelmina. Mrs. Fudge condemns them to the basement. A small one, however, from Bobby Pemberton (eighteen last March), with card attached, holds place upon the parlor table up to a very withered maturity.

As for Mr. Solomon Fudge, during this service, he exercises most praiseworthy attention; and shows such engrossment of thought—either in Dauphin or Doctrine—as is highly exemplary.

He commends and admires Dr. Muddleton, as a respectable and sound man, of healthy doctrine and unimpeachable character. He considers these opinions safe, and they bound his religious ideas. Dr. Muddleton does not give up his desk to begging agents, or any enthusiastic declaimers. Mr. Fudge does not trouble himself to inquire into the merits of any such haranguers—not he. He chooses to let well enough alone; and well enough in Christian matters seems to be written all over the person of Dr. Muddleton. His surplice, robe, manner and all seem to him the very incarnation of a good catholic faith. Indeed, an expression of opinion to this effect, to the clerical gentleman himself—when Mr. Fudge was a little maudlin with wine—met with no opposition on Dr. Muddleton's part.

Mr. Fudge is satisfied; Dr. Muddleton is satisfied; and for aught I know or believe, the Prince of Darkness, himself, is satisfied.

I am aware that these remarks are not in a fashionable vein. Fashion does not recognize intensity, either in faith or in manner. I should say that intensity, either in preaching, conversation, or habit, was vulgar and low-lived.

Presumptuous, wild people might picture to themselves a better livelihood and habit for Mrs. Fudge, daughter, son, and husband. They might imagine that a quiet modesty, charitable disposition, a careless submission to such superiority as Fashion bestows, a cultivation of the refinements rather than the enormities of life, might lend them more dignity, humanity, and contentment. This, however, is a prejudice of education.

Mrs. Fudge, reflecting upon her improved prospects, felicitating herself upon the effect of Wilhelmina's hat, and casting comparative glances around the very populous pews, suddenly caught a glimpse of a young gentleman, in company with the Spindles, whose appearance excited her keenest interest.

The Spindles, indeed, were rare people—subjects of considerable study, and not a little envy, with the Fudges. The Spindles appeared to have a natural aptitude for dress: some people seem born with all the adaptation to stays and stomachers which belongs to the revolving figures of those enterprising hair-dressers opposite Bond-street. The Spindles are among these. I doubt if the hair-dresser himself could have improved their figures in any respect for window-models. They are reputed very wealthy; their father being a heavy broker. They have a country-seat, speak French, polk liberally, and read the opera librettos from the Italian side.

It is natural that Mrs. Solomon Fudge should admire them (although she does talk about them outrageously); and it is, moreover, natural that she should feel a curious interest in the young gentleman, who was now luxuriating in what she considered as the very meridian of fashionable splendor.

Mrs. Fudge observes, after a series of reconnoitering glances (in which she is very careful not to catch the eye of the Spindles), that the young man is of a genteel figure; that his coat is remarkably short-tailed (excellent taste); that his cravat has the so-called Parisian tie; that his eye is mild, as if he were of a yielding temperament; and that his forehead, though somewhat low, is balanced by a very happy parting of the hair behind the head.

Miss Wilhelmina observes that he wears a large bunch of charms to his watch-chain; that his mouth is lighted up with a very lively-colored moustache; that he is of good height for a dancing-partner; that he pays little attention to the Miss Spindles (by which she judges him accustomed to elegant society); and, what pleases her still more, that he seems, by one or two eager glances thrown in her direction, to have a lively appreciation of her face.

Miss Wilhelmina concludes from these observations that he must be a delightful person; that he is probably not in love, at least not with the Spindles; and that he drives a fast trotter. Mrs. Fudge, on her part, decides that he is a young man of "good position," and possibly of expectations; at any rate, a very desirable acquaintance for herself and daughter. Mr. Fudge himself, if attention had been called to the young gentleman, would have indulged only in a pleasant comparison between young men generally, and his own dignity as former Mayor; from this he would have recurred to the sermon of his friend the Doctor, giving such earnestness to the hearing as would not interfere with a grateful and pervading sense of his own dignity and distinction.

There are those in the city who remember, some of them to their cost, an old brokerage firm of Spindle and Quid. Spindle and Quid held very high moneyed rank; their dealings at the board were extensive. Embarrassments, however, after a time, ensued: assignments were made in a quiet, orderly way; Mrs. Spindle, of course, retaining her house, carriage, and opera-box; and the creditors generally retaining the paper of Spindle and Quid. Arrangements, however, were soon made for a renewal of business under the name of Ezekiel Spindle; Quid retiring. All claims upon the firm were referred to Mr. Quid, who had retired, no one knew where. The credits of the firm were managed by Mr. Spindle, as agent for the old house.

It is supposed by many that an understanding still exists between Spindle and Quid, although of what precise nature it is impossible to say. Wall street partnerships are generally somewhat involved. Too searching a curiosity is found only to increase the fog which belongs to such arrangements, and sometimes even to dissolve the firm altogether. The fact, however, that some connection still existed, seemed to be confirmed by the easy circumstances in which young Quid—no other than the short-coated gentleman already subjected to Mrs. Fudge's observation—appeared to move

Outsiders and simple-minded persons, knowing only that Mr. Quid, senior, if he still existed, was a broken broker, would have wondered at the pleasant and affluent style in which Mr. Quid, junior, was observed to amble along upon the high-road of life. There are many young men about town, I observe, who suggest similar wonder. Young Quid has just returned from a European tour. He is clearly a man of the world: he is a member of a metropolitan club, at which his dues are very much cut down by a happy knack he possesses at whist or *écarté*. He has an eye for the arts; reasons well upon the comparative merits of ballet-dancers, and has his room set off with several naked statuettes of agreeable proportions, arranged upon plaster brackets. He has also prettily-engraved portraits of the horse Bostona, of Lady Suffolk, and of Celeste. His books are various; numbering a paper-covered Tom Jones, apparently much read; a well-bound Youatt on the Dog; a copy of Count d'Orsay, of Lalla Rookh, and a small volume of poetical quotations. He has also a French and Italian phrase-book; he is on familiar terms with some of the better-known barbers of the town, and will sometimes crack a word or two of Italian in their company; not extending, however, usually beyond "*buon giorno,*" or "*una ragazza dulcissima.*"

He is fond of mentioning incidentally his dinners

at the *Trois Frères*, or the *Café de Paris*, and his adventures, of a very superior character, at the *Ranelagh*, or the *Bal masqué*. The countesses he has met with on these occasions are exceedingly numerous; and the tears they must have shed at his desertion are almost frightful to contemplate. He has also a large and glowing record of similar adventures (reserved for the ear of his particular friends) in his own comparatively new country.

He enjoys the acquaintance of sundry English and French gentlemen, but not, as I am aware, of any Hungarians or Poles. His sympathies are wide, but aristocratic. He sometimes dines with a Londoner at the club, an agent, possibly, for some Manchester print-house, who pretends to a familiarity with steeple-chases, who has followed Sir Ralph Dingley's hounds down in Kent, and who has sometimes taken a tandem drive to the races, on a Derby day.

Mrs. Fudge remembers that her cousin Truman has had commercial dealings with the house of Spindle. She sees in this connection a channel opening toward gracious interviews, and congratulates herself in advance upon the attachment of so distinguished a young gentleman as Master Quid to the train of the youthful Wilhelmina.

And this is the way she worships.

IX.

Kitty and her New Friends.

"King James used to call for his old shoes. They were easiest for his feet. So, old friends are often the best."

Selden.

IT is pleasant to revert again to the modest and gentle face of our little friend Kitty. My inclination will draw me toward her, away from the soberer subjects of my story, very often.

For three or four days she has been in the great city, wondering, admiring, half sorrowing through it all. It is so new; it is so strange! The noise is so great, the people so many, the houses are so tall!

The Fudges have received her kindly. At least the widow Fudge, who is such a neat, quiet, old lady, in black bombazine, with such white collar and cuffs; and her hair, half grey, is so neatly parted under a very snowy cap; and then she has such a kind way—kissing little Kitty first upon the forehead and then upon the cheek; and then, as if that were not enough, taking her head between her hands, and kissing her fairly and honestly, just where such a face as Kitty's should be kissed.

Beside all, the widow Fudge is such a housekeeper, with such capital servants, and everything seems just in the place it should be in, and as if dirt and disorder could not possibly come near the prim widow Fudge!

It has frequently struck me that such ladies of the old school of house-keepers are always in the luck of finding good servants; whereas, your slatternly, half-and-half people are always quarrelling about their slut of a Betty, or a filthy serving-man.

The girls, Jemima and Bridget (rather old girls, to be sure), are delighted with Kitty. They frolic around her like playful cats, one seizing her mantilla, and the other her hat; and again, her gloves, and her little fur-trimmed over-shoes, and her muff, until nothing is left of Kitty but her grey travelling-dress and her own sweet face and figure. Thereupon nothing is to be done but to kiss over again (they were not to be blamed), and again and again, until Kitty was perfectly exhausted of kisses;

utterly rifled, with no strength to receive kisses any longer ; much less to kiss back again.

Whether a little of all this was not undertaken to pique the worthy Truman Bodgers, Esquire, who stood by with a very lackadaisical expression—sometimes screwing up his mouth, from very sympathy, into a kissing shape—I cannot tell. I know it is not an unusual artifice to tease quiet bachelors.

Then, Kitty must be shown the room, and the house, and the little garden in the rear, and the new books, and the last year's presents, and the fall style of bonnet, and a new Kossuth work-bag, and a bottle of Alboni salts, besides a rich bit of crewel-work of Bridget's, which Jemima classically calls her *magnum opus*.

The new masters for Kitty are to be talked over. There is Monsieur Petit, a Parisian, who is a delightful little man, and always so cheerful. But he is not, perhaps, so good a teacher (at least Jemima, who is a judge of French, thinks so) as Mademoiselle Entrenous, who has been unfortunate ; was of a noble family; is reduced: and so lady-like, and with such a melancholy expression of countenance, that really Jemima quite pitied her, and had at one time conceived a sort of Damon-and-Pythias friendship for her, and written sonnets to her, which Mademoiselle, not being able to read, wept over.

As for music, there was Monsieur Hanstihizy, a delightful pale Pole, who sang bewitchingly, and all the girls were dying (so said Bridget) of love for him. He had been wounded, too—in some action, at some time, for some very patriotic cause. He was so conciliating, too; and explained the European pictures so well. Besides, he had been spoken of in the *Home Journal*, and was in the very best society.

Mrs. Solomon Fudge and Wilhelmina, perhaps to humor the regard of Mr. Bodgers, and perhaps from a sense of duty, made an early call upon Kitty in the claret carriage, with the white horses. The cousins had not met since they were girls together, years ago. Kitty could not but admire the step and manner of Wilhelmina, as she skipped from the carriage. The aunt and cousin dropped very elegant, patronizing kisses upon Kitty's forehead as they met her ; hoping she was well, and thinking she looked *very* well ; and hoping her mamma was well, interrupted by a sigh from Mrs. Fudge, and a melancholy ejaculation of "Poor Susy!" in a tone which might have led a stranger to suppose that her sister Susy was indeed a very miserable creature.

The aunt and cousin were glad to see Kitty, they said ; and hoped she would enjoy herself—in a way that made Kitty very much fear she never should. Never had Kitty seen such a silk as her Aunt Solomon was wearing: Aunt Solomon surmised this, at least, from the expression of Kitty's eyes, and it pleased her. She felt her heart warming toward Kitty. Never had Kitty seen such a magnificent bonnet as her cousin happened to be wearing; and although she contained her admiration, Wilhelmina saw it, and felt an inclination toward Kitty in consequence.

It was a matter of additional surprise to our country friend that Bridget and Jemima wore a very subdued and dignified air in the presence of Aunt Solomon: and furthermore, that they were by no means so *empressées* in their manner toward Wilhelmina as toward herself; a fact which will puzzle her very much less when she comes to see more of the world. Mrs. and Miss Fudge would be very happy to see Kitty at their house, and if convenient, Bridget and Jemima. At all which, Kitty, in her naïve manner, expressed herself very thankful, and "would surely come." The Misses Fudge, on the other hand, "would be very happy," but looked as if they meant quite differently.

Now, with all the love that Kitty feels she ought to bear toward her Aunt Solomon and Wilhelmina, she certainly does experience relief at their leave-taking; and she thinks of them, thinking as kindly as she can, "Elegant ladies:" nothing more can come to Kitty's thought. Courage! Mrs. Fudge and daughter; you are driving hard in your claret carriage toward elegant society!

There are neighbors of the Misses Bridget and Jemima, to whom I have already alluded; especially the retired grocer opposite. Neither of the young ladies speak of this gentleman to Kitty—a remarkable and significant fact.

Their landlord, however, and next-door neighbor, Kitty has met. He was said at one time to show attention to Jemima: he probably did not continue such attention for a long time, as will be inferred from his usual very characteristic dispatch, herein exhibited.

His name is Blimmer. Mr. Blimmer is an enterprising, indefatigable, middle-aged, voluble man. He is the founder and chief proprietor of that elegant new town, called Blimmersville, "delightfully situated upon the shores of Long Island Sound, at an easy distance from the business part of the city, and offering a quiet rural home to those whose avocations or inclinations induce them to leave behind them, for a while, the dust and heat of the city, and to enjoy the salubriousness of a rarefied country air, convenient to accessible salt-water bathing." (I have ventured to quote, in this connection, a few paragraphs from Mr. Blimmer's own programme.) "A town, it may be remarked, which is yet honored with but two small and tasteful suburban residences, but which is on the highway to prosperity, and will soon be adorned with a multitude of desirable houses, from the costly mansions of the opulent to the tasteful humility of the small trader, interspersed with graceful churches, and with shops, for all such as prefer to buy their groceries in the country."

Mr. Blimmer is an active man—a very active man. He is never easy, unless under pressure. He keeps the steam up. If he sits down, he twirls the chair next him, and talks. If he stands, he gesticulates violently, and talks. If he rides, he threshes the reins upon his beast, emphasizes with his elbows, and talks. He has no charity and no fellow-feeling for men who sit still. He has always a pocket full of papers, half of them programmes, and has always a fuller schedule, more satisfactory, at the office. He is always on the way to Blimmersville, or just arrived from Blimmersville. He cuts his beefsteak into town-lots, and dines and digests Blimmersville. He is familiar with many subjects, and talks with great glibness; he makes every subject bear on Blimmersville. His main object in life is to interest people in Blimmersville; not for the sake of profit, but because satisfied that no man in the world can be thoroughly happy without buying a lot and building a suburban mansion (plans furnished gratis) at Blimmersville. His advertisements are in every ferry-boat, and his longings are in every breeze that wafts toward Blimmersville.

He seeks to interest clergymen in the growth of a new town, where the delights and purity of Eden will be revived. He offers the clergymen lots (very eligible) at half-price; and shows, upon the diagram, the probable site of the church of Blimmersville.

Mr. Blimmer meets Kitty gladly: he always meets strangers gladly. He wishes to know if her mother or father (if living) think of moving into the neighborhood of the city? He should be gratified, some pleasant day, in accompanying her, with her friends Bridget and Jemima, to Blimmersville. He thinks they would be interested in viewing the site: "a lovely spot, embracing wide ocean-views, charming expanse of lawn, interspersed with diversified copses shading the meadows, where may be seen at certain seasons the lowing kine."

Kitty conceives, from the character of Mr. Blimmer, her first idea of metropolitan enterprise; very superior to good, quiet Uncle Bodgers; very to Harry Flint!

And Kitty is lost in admiration, after only three days of city life; in admiration of the shops, the people, the dresses—every thing!

Kitty leans in the twilight upon the back of her chair, with the hum of the noisy world coming in a great roar tó her ear. And Kitty thinks: yet very scattered, and wandering, and wayward is Kitty's thinking.

She thinks of Bridget: how prettily she works crewel: and if she is not old enough to be married; and if so, why she has never married; and if nobody ever loved her; and if nobody does love in cities (for shame, Kitty!) as they love in the country.

Kitty thinks of Jemima, the prim sister, and of the beautiful verses she writes; and why she has never heard of her verses in the papers; and if Miss Bremer could write better; and why (if men dared) Jemima too is not married.

Kitty thinks of Wilhelmina, and of her white hat trimmed with gorgeous jonquils, and of the sensation she would make in Newtown, and of the small sensation she creates here; and she wonders how much feeling (if any) is at the bottom of all her manner, and if she could love a kind old mother like hers, or the neighbors' little children, as she loves them. Then, this thought seems wrong to Kitty, and she tries to blot it out, but she cannot.

Kitty thinks of Mrs. Fudge in her morning-wrapper of such extraordinary colors, and of her hand buried in lace, and looking smaller for the burial, and wonders if this is accidental; and she thinks of her soft carpets, and of her evening-dress, laced as it was painfully, and wonders if Mrs. Fudge is, after all, so very, very happy.

Kitty thinks of her dignified Uncle Solomon, with his white cravat, and his gold-bowed spectacles, and his even, measured gait, and of his grunted replies to his wife's questionings, and of his champagne at dinner; and she tries hard to fancy how grand it must be to become a great man in the city.

Kitty thinks of her Uncle Truman, and of that kind manner of his: always kind through all his roughness. She recalls pleasantly his good-by; and how he lingered, and pressed her hand very hard, and said, "Kiss me, Kit."

And how she did.

And how he said, "Kiss me again, Kit," and how she kissed him again; and after that, he walked away slowly, always in that queer old brown surtout; but it wrapped, she thought, the warm heart of a good man. And she feels in her pocket for the little purse he had filled so well; and not for this, save only as a token, her heart warms toward Truman Bodgers.

Then Kitty thinks of her mother, alone, in the old house. Oh, sadly alone! Kitty's thought dies here into a half-sob. The twilight deepens in the room, and Kitty peoples the coming evening with old friends;—wandering with them again through the walks by the old homestead;—picking roses, eyeing Harry Flint; twisting roses, talking with Harry Flint; eating roses, listening to Harry Flint; dropping roses,—all in the twilight, by the dear old homestead!

And Kitty saddens with the floating thoughts, and bows her head lower and lower upon the back of her chair, until sleep creeps over her weary eyes and brain; and a tangled vision drifts across her dream, of Mr. Bodgers in a blue coat, with heavy golden buttons; and of Harry Flint, in Solomon Fudge's white cravat; and of Mrs. Fudge and daughter, driving in a claret-colored coach, on the way toward Heaven.

X.

PARIS EXPERIENCE OF WASH. FUDGE.

"OH! had a man of daring spirit, of genius, penetration, and learning, travelled to that city, what might not mankind expect! How would he enlighten the region to which he travelled, and what a variety of knowledge and useful improvement would he not bring back in exchange!"

GOLDSMITH.

GEO. WASHINGTON FUDGE admires Paris. It would be strange if he did not admire Paris. But in his view, it adds considerably to the reputation of Paris, that he, Wash. Fudge, does admire it. It has the same effect, he does not doubt, upon his mother's appreciation of Paris. Of his father's notions he is not so confident.

He has left his attic in the Hotel Meurice, and has taken apartments across the water, upon the

Quai Voltaire. He is in the fourth story, and is occupant of a charming salon, and chamber attached. The waxed stairways and the brick floors astonish him. The gilt clock that ticks upon his mantel, the magnificent pier-table, the mirrors, and the lounges delight him. He feels, too, a warm regard for the old lady in horn spectacles, who sits every day in the porter's lodge, who gives him such a friendly *bon jour*, and who never quarrels either with his hours or his visitors.

As for his hours, he rounds them by what he reckons the polite standard. At eleven of the morning, the old lady below serves him with a roll, a cup of coffee, a little plate of radishes and of butter. All these he dispatches leisurely, and finishes his toilet by half-past twelve. He then indulges himself in a ramble over the bridge and through the garden of the Tuileries. He is much struck with the architectural effect of the palace, and describes it in a friendly letter to his mother as "a magnificent specimen of long and high-roofed architecture in stone." He indulges in home-comparisons of the fountains, and avenues of trees, not wholly favorable to Grammercy Park. He strolls to that angle of the terrace where he yesterday encountered a very coquettish grisette; and not finding her, he consoles himself with a chair, and with a careless observation of the carriages, and mounted guards, and women and children trooping across the Place de la Concorde.

Sauntering afterward through the avenue of the Champs Elysées, he encounters a vivacious talker, who invites him, in the blandest manner, to try a shot or two at a revolving company of clay images. Washington being, as I said, of a liberal nature, advances half a franc, which is good for four shots, and counts on securing one of the prizes in the shape of a paste gew-gaw for his old friend of the *conciergerie.* He fires his successive discharges without damaging in the least the little plaster Cupids, who continue their quiet revolutions as before.

His next venture of the morning is in pistol-practice upon the heart of a very brigand-looking figure, which traverses a wild scene of canvas and pine boards, at five sous the transit. Washington having failed as before, continues his entertainment by gazing over the shoulders of two short soldiers, at the extraordinary tricks of an accomplished juggler, who picks up pieces of two sous with a staff, and who suggests a farther trial upon silver coin; which being offered by Mr. Fudge, is at once transferred in a graceful manner to the juggler's pocket, amid the plaudits of the two short soldiers.

Mr. Fudge is farther attracted by the saltambic

feats of a young lady in an exceedingly short blue velvet dress, who is surrounded by a ring of admiring soldiers, and accompanied in her *poses* by fiddle and clarionet. Washington patronizes the performance by a liberal cast of small coins, and is rewarded by a gracious smile from the young lady in the short velvet dress.

At this juncture he recalls an engagement with his Professor of the English and French languages. The Professor has rooms at the top of a house in the Rue St. Honoré. He keeps a parrot and a cat—maltese color; and has farther graced his apartment with two or three lively statuettes of famous dancing characters. He is sixty years, or thereabout, and takes snuff liberally; although he still wears varnished boots, and talks freely of his brilliant intrigues. He furthermore instructs Mr. Fudge in execrable English about his connection with the various revolutions of France, and his hair-breadth escapes. He listens kindly to such confidential disclosures as Mr. Fudge is pleased to make in regard to his friends and family. He indulges in a strain of political and philosophic reflections which satisfy Washington Fudge that the Professor has been a man sadly overlooked in the distribution of the administrative functions. He hints as much to the old lady in the porter's lodge, who shrugs her shoulders, and says, "*Possible!*"

At six, he smokes a cigar over a small cup of coffee, outside the Rotunde of the Palais Royale; ogling meantime, through the window, the very bewitching young lady who presides over the tables, the spoons, and the sugar. He afterward luxuriates, in company with his friend, in a cab-drive along the Boulevard and the Quai, terminating at the brilliantly-illuminated entrance of a hall in the Rue St. Honoré. Upon the payment of two francs, he is here ushered into a scene of bewildering magnificence. A band of eighty performers is discoursing music from a gay pavilion, decorated with tri-color, in the centre of the *salle*. Gas-lights are casting through orange and purple reflectors, hues innumerable. The floor is trembling under the tread of a hundred coupled waltzers, and the galleries above and below are swimming with eyes, fans, and feathers.

It is needless to say that young Mr. Fudge pursues his habit of observation in such quarters, with all his accustomed alacrity; he even addresses one or two brother Americans, whom he encounters in the course of the evening, in French; but, upon being pressed in that language, recovers his recollection, and resumes his native tongue.

Mr. Fudge observes, from the habit of his companions, that the young ladies present are not averse to wine—if mingled with water ; he farther observes that they do not resent, with any air of disdain, such attentions as strangers may be disposed to offer, in a spirit of kindness ; they also courteously relieve the foreigner of those embarrassments which naturally belong to one unacquainted with the customs and language of the country.

In short, Mr. Fudge is delighted with the adventures of the evening, and goes home in a maudlin state.

It is my opinion that this day's experience of my young friend Wash. Fudge is quite similar to that of most of the very young men who are sent to Paris with a view of completing their education, and establishing a position in polite society. It is my opinion that many such stolid papas as Mr. Solomon Fudge, wrapped up in an impenetrable sense of their own foresight and prudence, are meantime cherishing the confirmed belief that their hopeful sons are acquiring a large acquaintance with the language and public policy of the country, and are reaping such advantages from foreign travel as will advance highly their interests in the commercial or political world.

And it is my farther opinion, that many such

aspiring mothers as Mrs. Solomon Fudge, indulge in the pleasing reflection that their darling Wash. Fudges are equipping themselves with every polite accomplishment, becoming absolute masters of all Parisian finesse, whether of language or manner, and disturbing cruelly, by their various charms and playful *equivoques*, the tender affections of all the marriageable daughters of all the titled ladies of Paris.

[The mother will live long enough yet, to find her poor pride cut to the quick, by the children on whose training she poises her worldly—and only—hope. And the stately Solomon Fudge, with all the dignity of his past honors crusted on him, and the stiffness of his stock-list, and his haughtiness of look, may yet find that the worldly and golden armor he wears, with such clanking and glitter, has in it weakly jointures, whereat the arrows of sorrow and of mortification may drive (possibly from a filial hand), and pierce through to his old, seared heart, making his high manhood wilt, like grass that is cut in June!]

In a genial and flowing humor, Mr. Fudge communicates with an old boon-companion of the city: He is *not* disappointed in the masked balls—not in the least. They are quite up to his mark; altogether splendid affairs. "You have to fancy all the orchestras of your city tuning together to a 'tip-top polka;' and a thousand figures, more or less, in brown, grey, blue and gold spangles; young and old ones; big noses and little ones; everything hobgoblin and ghostly; and all of them polking as if the deuce was in them. Such tidy grisettes, too, and such pretty figures as they show *en garçon!* Have not indulged much myself upon the floor: they have an awkward way of tossing their feet into one's face, which is embarrassing; beside which, had my hat once or twice crushed over my eyes—supposed to be done by a tall *Pierrot* in steeple-crowned hat and long sleeves, who looked very sanctimoniously.

"Kept mostly to the *salon*, among the better class of ladies; am fully satisfied that some among them were of quite a superior order; indeed, as much was hinted to me by the ladies themselves; am obliged to keep very dark; French husbands are an excessively jealous people. Held some intensely interesting conversations; am naturally improving in French—quite at home indeed. Having a rendezvous at the Grand Opera at nine o'clock, must close hastily. Hope the boys are well."

Under such pleasant auspices, Mr. Fudge finds the winter slipping away at a very comfortable pace. He is expressing as much to himself, in a consolatory way, over his egg and roll, on a fine February morning, when the old lady from below taps at his door, and hands him a very delicate-looking note, slightly odorous of a subdued and lady-like perfume. The hand, too, is fair and graceful—wholly unknown to Mr. Fudge; and surprises and delights him with the following challenge:

"*M. Fudge est prié de se rendre ce soir, au bal masqué, à minuit et demi, à la rencontre d'un domino noir.*"

To say merely that Mr. Fudge determined to be present at the masked ball at the time designated, would convey but a small idea of the ardor and enthusiasm of his character. He elaborated his toilet to a degree that to most men would have been painful. His coiffeur surpassed himself. Mr. Fudge fairly languished for the hour to arrive.

It is needless to add that he was punctual. He encountered the Domino. He passed up and down the corridors, and through the *salon*, with that graceful figure leaning upon his arm: nor was it the grace alone that fired him, but the piquancy of her talk—catching his broken sentences, and rounding them into fullness; anticipating his thought; unriddling his half-expressed surprises; provoking him with her knowledge of his history and family; lifting her finger in warning against all his eagerness to solve the mystery; discoursing philosophically upon the scene before them; dropping half sentences of English, and complimenting his French, in a way that sets poor Wash. Fudge altogether beside himself.

To make the matter still worse, his new acquaintance, contrary, as he believes, to all precedent, insists that Mr. Fudge shall make no attempt to track her from the ball: her reasons for all the mystery are so vague and shadowy as to pique his curiosity the more.

Finally, at three of the morning, after a half-exacted promise to appear again, she glides away from him into the throng of Dominos, and is lost.

To Mr. Fudge this is a new and delightful experience; indeed, on comparing it with the past experience of Parisian acquaintances, he regards it as altogether unique, and appreciates his success and good fortune accordingly. He reëxamines very scrutinizingly their very brief correspondence. It is clearly a lady-like hand—a refined hand, so to speak. He ventures to submit it to the eye of the distinguished gentleman, his professor of languages. The Professor is curious, very; he thinks Mr. Fudge fortune's favorite (which Mr. Fudge privately confirms), and is satisfied both of the station and dignity of his correspondent. He farther remarks that Mr. Fudge is a dangerous fellow; and he doubts if he is doing his duty in perfecting him to any greater degree in the finesse of the language.

The knowledge which the unknown lady appears to possess of Mr. Fudge's history and family somewhat surprises him; not that such things might not very properly and naturally be known to the European world; but since he has found that in the majority of instances such facts were *not* known. His banker, being a bachelor, is relieved of the suspicion which might otherwise attach to his wife or daughters.

In this connection, however, the thought of young Mr. Fudge reverts suddenly to the once admired but now neglected Miss Jenkins. Miss Jenkins is still in Paris; Miss Jenkins' figure corresponded well with that of the domino; Miss Jenkins' interesting manner might easily he thought, under the excitement of the masquerade, ripen into that coquettish tenderness which he had found so beguiling. Miss Jenkins, moreover, was familiar, to some extent, with his family history, and with his aims in life. He had been cruelly inattentive to Miss Jenkins: Miss Jenkins was now taking the revenge of an affectionate and injured woman.

With this thought fastening itself by degrees

firmly upon his mind, Mr. Washington Fudge, without the least touch of pity for feeble hearts in his air or manner, throws back his coat-collar upon his shoulders, inserts his thumbs in the arm-holes of his waistcoat, and placing himself in a fancy attitude before the mirror, indulges himself in a long, low, cheerful whistle.

XI.

Squire Bodgers at Home.

> "He covets less
> Than misery itself would give; rewards
> His deeds with doing them: and is content
> To spend the time to end it." Shakspeare.

THE village of Newtown is as pretty a place as one can find in a ten days' drive around the city of New York. It smacks of the old and quiet times when gossips herded at the village inn, and when, once or twice in the year, the whole country around thronged upon the green to some travelling show. It has its deacons and squires; it has its branching elms, throwing their trembling shadows across the village street; it has an humble parsonage-house, all embowered with many cherry-trees, and a gigantic butternut: it has its country store, with its black-topped posts, where the farmers' wives "hitch their colts;" and with its strange variety of crockery, calicoes, teas, and molasses. There is the head clerk, with a pen behind his ear, deeply immersed in calculations; and with fingers sticky with keg-raisins. There is the store-keeper himself, a stout, bland man, with wristbands turned up, who tries his groceries upon the tip of his fore-finger, and wipes his finger upon the nether portion of his dress, until his pantaloons, from the hip to the knee, have become cheerfully glazed with a shining and unctuous mixture of lamp-oil, rosin, lamp-black, spirits of turpentine, and New Orleans sugar.

The town has its tailor—over the store: with a sign-board on which is a gilt pair of shears; and a last year's plate of the fashions is in the window. He possesses a ready disposition to have his customers' work done on Saturday night, except "his girls" are taken sick—which usually occurs. There is also the shoemaker, in a quiet, small, rather close-smelling shop, by himself; who "taps" for half the city price, and who always keeps his word, except he is out of "luvor"—which sometimes happens.

Two attorneys, who once did business under the general firm of Bivins and Rip, have, by mutual consent, dissolved partnership; and henceforth attend to the law-business in all its details, such as drawing of writs and leases, collection of moneys, etc., at their respective offices: Timothy Rip, first door to the right, above Miss Doolittle's millinery-store; and Ebenezer Bivins, at the old stand on the meeting-house corner.

There are also sundry old-fashioned houses scattered through the little town: houses with gamble-roofs, and mossy, mouldy-looking, dormer-windows; houses with gray-stone chimneys, on which some ancient date is inscribed in the quaint-shaped letters which you see in old primers; houses with clambering vines that seem as old as the houses, and ready with their weight of leaves to crush the walls they cling to, or if need be, to bury them under a cloak of green: there are houses in out-of-the-way places with strange-shaped hipped roofs, about which lurk ancient tales of Dutch or Puritan wrong; floors spotted with blood (not to be washed out with the hardest scrubbing); haunted houses, pointed at of school-boys, and romantic misses in gingham aprons.

The village is old, as I said; and lying out of the reach of railway enterprise, has fallen sadly in the wake of modern progress. Two sawmills upon the brook above the village have stopped.

The long-store is positively closed. Squire Bivins' practice has fallen off, they say, at least one-third. But two house-raisings have been known within the town-limits in the last three years; no new barn has been erected, with the exception of an addition to Smith's livery-stable. Even the tan-works, belonging to the gentleman on whose account solely I have entered upon this long digression—I speak of Truman Bodgers, Esquire—are in a dilapidated condition, and exhibit undoubted evidences of dissolution.

Squire Bodgers is owner and occupant of one of the houses to which I have alluded. His house is an old house, and a gamble-roofed house. Hollyhocks and red roses are growing (during summer) beside the path that leads to his door. Ancestral trees hang over the mossy roof. Although living in such a quiet, decayed town, Squire Bodgers has had the shrewdness to perceive, and to avail himself of the commercial drift of the day. He has had the courage—for the want of which many such old-fashioned men have become poverty-stricken—to withdraw his capital from the sluggish, narrowing channels, and to bestow it upon the growing enterprise of the cities. The result is, that Mr. Bodgers is a rich man; richer than most people suppose him; and far richer than Mrs.

Solomon Fudge, amid all her condescension of manner, has for one moment imagined.

Upon the day on which this chapter of the Fudge record is supposed to open, Mr. Truman Bodgers is sitting before the fire, in a comfortable high-backed chair, in what he calls the library, under the roof of the antique mansion I have briefly described. Two portraits are hanging on the wall, over which the eyes of Mr. Bodgers occasionally glance, with a pleasantly mournful expression. One of them is that of a hale old gentleman, long since gone, who was the builder of the mansion, and the father of the present occupant. The other picture shows a kindly old lady's smile, which was half ruined by blindness twenty-odd years ago; and which only went out finally twelve months since, when the old lady (Mr. Bodgers' mother) died.

Being blind, she loved greatly to listen to pleasant voices, reading out of pleasant books; and Kitty Fleming, having such a voice as made even dull books pleasant, won her way deeply into the old lady's regard, and at the same time into the affections of her son. She was as dear, I am sure, to the old lady as would have been any grandchild, and had grown as dear to the son as any daughter; perhaps she was even dearer.

I have said that these two pictures hung upon the walls of Mr. Bodgers' room. There was a third picture, much smaller than the other two, in a little drawer of the antique secretary which stood just at his elbow. It was in a morocco case, and few ever opened it, save Mr. Bodgers himself. It was the miniature of a sweet-faced girl—not Kitty, or Kitty's mother.

Mr. Bodgers even now is dwelling on it mournfully. An old affection lingers about that picture of a beauty long since gone to the world of spirits. Even Squire Bodgers, under that rough exterior, has his tender places, and his affections flowing like a river—widely and vainly. The world is altogether too apt to consign the withered hulk of the bachelor who has seen his five-and-fifty years to the tomb of all passionate feeling. It is my honest opinion that bachelors, thoroughly ripened in years, are the most kind, tender, affectionate, hopeful, self-denying, and calumniated creatures that are to be found in the world.

Did people but know the seared hopes and brimming expectancies which struggle, "fierce as youth," in the breasts of such men, they would judge more wisely. Providence has dealt kindly with us all. And as the fountains of hope dry up along the straitened waste of the years that are to come, deep wells of holy and sainted memories gush to the light behind us, and freshen us—to tears!

There is a paquet of faded letters in a pigeon-hole of the antique secretary, which, if run over in the careful way in which our friend Mr. Bodgers runs them over on some late nights in winter, would unfold the history of the minature. It is, after all, only the old story of love, blighted by the Destroyer long ago, and sometimes carrying back the manly heart, by desperate leaps, over the wide gap which thirty years open in life.

It is not often, however, that the practical Mr. Bodgers wanders back so far; it is not often that he looks over, so wistfully as now, the faded paquet of letters; it is not often that he lingers, when the sun is shining so cheerfully as it is, by his desk and his fireside.

The truth is, Mr. Bodgers has met this day with one of those little accidents which might easily have been a large one, and which wakens the thought of Fatality; and makes a serious man balance the remaining weight of his days. Therefore it is that the shattered arm, in a sling, has kept Mr. Bodgers by his desk, and by the old letters and pictures, with half-mournful thought. And in virtue of the same mishap, his reflections have turned upon testamentary documents, and upon his list of rentals, and upon the chance—perhaps a sudden chance—that all he now calls his own, will lie bound up soon in some short testamentary parchment. And therefore it is that such old parchments have come under his eye this day; and with the parchments, the cherished letters; and with the letters, the pictures; and with the pictures, the vague and shadowy memories; and with the memories—that moistened eye.

Then the eye falls upon the parchments again, as if for relief; and Mr. Bodgers thinks—of his own Will.

"It must be drawn," says Mr. Bodgers, talking to himself.

"As well now as ever," says Mr. Bodgers, thrusting his papers into a pigeon-hole.

"It shall be done this very day," says Mr. Bodgers, giving emphasis to the remark by three consecutive taps upon the lid of his snuff-box.

A half-hour after, and the careless spectator might have observed a solitary individual, with a brown surtout thrown over his shoulder, and his right arm slung in a yellow bandanna, marching with a resolute step into the office of Squire 'Nezer Bivins, at his old stand, upon the meeting-house corner.

XII.

Squire Bodgers Makes a Will.

"There is no fooling with life, when it is once turned beyond forty; the seeking of a fortune then is but a desperate after-game: it is a hundred to one if a man fling two sixes, and recover all."

Cowley.

IT is a disagreeable thing for a bachelor to make his will. He is disposed to put it off to a very late day. It implies a certain hopelessness of any nearer ties to kindred than belong to his present lonely estate. It is a tacit acknowledgment that the world of feeling has waned; that the hazards of youth have been fruitless; that the path lies straight, and short, to the end. No man likes to feel this; still less does he like to act as if he felt it.

It is a sad thing that a man cannot carry a few ten per cent. paying stocks out of the world with him. It would be a great relief to many of our brokers and capitalists. It would soften the way of a vast many people to the grave. It would excite brilliant expectations. I think I know of several, ladies and gentlemen, who, in that event, might hope to "make a sensation," in the other world.

I may venture to say, however, that such a thing cannot be done. If the transfer could be accomplished anywhere, it could be accomplished in Wall street. It cannot be done in Wall street. And the worst of the matter is, that we do not find out the impossibility of the thing, until we come very near to the jumping-off place. Then, when the melancholy truth forces itself upon us, that all our stocks will be at a cent. per cent. discount in the other world, we conceive the idea of being generous. It would be an odd sort of generosity, if it were not so very popular.

To return, however, to Mr. Truman Bodgers: there was a strong reason for his making his will, independent of any mistrust he might have about carrying his property with him. Without a will, his estate, which, as I have already hinted, is large, would follow the leading of the law, and revert to certain heirs, about whom Mr. Bodgers knew nothing.

To explain this extraordinary circumstance, which, I frankly confess, seems more like a fiction of the novel-writers than the simple incident of a family narrative, I must be suffered to go back a step or two in the history of Mr. Bodgers.

Mr. Bodgers had a brother much older than himself, who died long ago. This brother, very much against the wish of old Mr. Bodgers, had married a dashing lady of the town, who survived him in a long and blooming widowhood, relieved by the presence of one little girl, and by the added charms of a life in Paris. The old gentleman being a sturdy disciplinarian, and having cut off the son, was very little disposed to follow the widow to Paris. Indeed, report said she led an evil life, and that, under a changed name, she gave herself up to such of the gayeties of French life as are very apt to play the mischief with a self-indulgent woman.

My hero, Truman Bodgers, grew up with very little knowledge of his elder brother, and with far less of the widow; who, long before the younger brother had arrived at manhood, had disappeared, under her assumed name, in the coteries of the German springs. Rumor had whispered several times of the marriage of the daughter to some needy American adventurer; but the alliance was not one which would warrant boastfulness, even in an adventurer. The whole connection had long ago proved itself an unwelcome one to Mr. Bodgers, and it is not strange that he should banish it from his thought in the drafting of his will.

Having thus cleared up, so far as I am able, this bit of family history, I take the liberty of introducing Ebenezer Bivins, Esq., legal adviser of Mr. Bodgers, and Justice of the Peace.

Mr. Bivins is a lean, lank man, in silver-bowed spectacles, and a snuff-colored wig. His spectacles ordinarily repose a long way down upon the bridge of a very sharp nose, yet cheerfully red. His wig is stiff, and glides off over a somewhat greasy coat-collar, in one of those graceful curves which belong to the sheet-iron roofs of a Chinese veranda. He has sharp speech, and a sharp laugh, although a very self-possessed one.

He has a respect for Newtown, as the home and birth-place of Mr. Bivins; he has a respect for the world and for nature, as having been the play-ground and the nurse of Mr. Bivins, when in infancy. He has a respect for summer, since it is a season which allows Mr. Bivins to economize in fuel; he has a respect, too, for winter, since it is a season which allows Mr. Bivins to enjoy that triumph over the elements and nature, which his foresight and prudence have prepared.

You would naturally (and correctly) suppose him to be the father of a lean young lady, of hopeless maidenhood and sharp voice, who is extremely neat, who wears a quilted petticoat of yellow and red, who delights in boxing the ears of the small boys of her class in Sunday-school, and who boasts the name of Mehitabel Bivins.

It has always been a wonder to me, and I dare say always will be, how any woman in the world could commit the absurdity of ever loving such a man as Ebenezer Bivins, or indeed any one of that class of men. It has cost me serious reflection. How is it possible, I have thought, for a woman to fondle, in the loving way the poets speak of, a man in a snuff-colored wig, projecting at such a sharp angle, over a greasy coat-collar? How can it be possible to kindle any romantic enthusiasm about such a peaked, red-colored nose, or such threadbare pantaloons, so short in the legs?

Yet Mr. Bivins and Mrs. Bivins have no doubt had their poetic transports; they have loved, been coy, advanced, retreated, cooed, kissed, and been married, like all the rest of the world. Still, I cannot forbear wondering. I waste a great deal of wonder in the same way. I am not ambitious of becoming the subject of a similar wonder.

Mr. Bivins is sitting before an open wood-fire, where two or three sticks are smouldering sulkily, throwing out a little smoke over the front of the stove, and a little smoke out of the stove-joints (poorly calked with burnt putty), and a little more smoke out of the easy scape-hole to the chimney. The tall book-case, with its reports and statutes, is comfortably browned with smoke ; and the baize-topped desk, and the leather-bottomed chairs, and the round interest-table hanging on the wall, and the Christian Almanac, and the cotton umbrella in the corner, and the snuff-colored-wig of Mr. Bivins, all smell of smoke.

The ashes in the stove are crusted over, and honey-combed, like volcanic tufa, with old discharges of tobacco-juice ; and the andirons show ancient, ashy drapery, formed by the continuous tobacco-drip of gone-by days and months. A few russet apple-parings and cores, half covered with soot, relieve the volcanic aspect of the ashes ; and a broken ink-bottle rises from the débris, like some monument of art amid the ruins of Pompeii.

Mr Bivins is most happy to see Squire Bodgers. He removes his spectacles, gives his pantaloons a toilet hitch in a downward direction, and passing his hand with a rapid precautionary movement over the surface of his wig, throws himself back in his chair, with an air, as much as to say, "You are welcome, Mr. Bodgers, for a handsome consideration, to the present employ of the superior legal acquirements of Squire Bivins."

Mr. Bodgers draws up his chair, touches Mr. Bivins upon the knee, and drops a quiet gesture toward a young man busily writing in the corner.

"Ah, Mr. Flint, will you be kind enough to step into the inner office for a few moments?"

Mr. Flint retires to the inner office; but the partition is thin; and busy as he tries to make himself with his own thoughts, the frequent mention of Kitty Fleming, coupled with "thousands," and "seven per cents.," and "event of her death," and "event of my death," and "Mrs. Fleming," disturbs him very strangely.

The truth is, Mr. Harry Flint, for this is no other, with few friends in the world, living with an old aunt, and having none to care for, save a sweet wee bit of a sister who clings to him every morning, and who welcomes him every evening with a pair of snowy little arms, and a kiss—Harry Flint, I say, has been foolish enough to conceive a strong fondness for Kitty Fleming. He has done this, notwithstanding he has heard all the rumors about herself and Mr. Bodgers; he has done this, notwithstanding she has gone away to find new and more brilliant favorites in the city.

Entertaining such views, it is quite natural that he should be shocked, now that he comes to overhear, unintentionally, some of the details of the marriage settlement with Mr. Bodgers. Harry Flint is not without spirit, although he has passed his life in Newtown. Indeed, he has only lingered there through the influence of certain attachments, at which I have hinted.

He recalls now all Kitty's words, and her smiles, and her leave-taking, so gentle and tremulous; and he recalls all her little kindnesses to Bessie Flint (as if a good-hearted girl would do any less), and wonders if it all conveyed nothing of hope, nothing of trust, on which *he* might feed?

And old Mr. Bodgers—clumsy Bodgers (guard yourself, Harry Flint!) can it be?—can Kitty Fleming love him? Yet he is not so old; a ripe-hearted man; living proudly in the old paternal mansion: Kitty would honor it; Kitty would love it, perhaps. Kitty, Kitty! are these things worth more to you than the overflowing fondness of a young, strong-beating heart, aching to pour out its fullness of love?

Harry Flint walks back and forth across the inner office; and then he hearkens a moment.

"Kitty is a smart girl," says Squire Bivins.

"An angel," says Mr. Bodgers. And why should he not say it, Mr. Harry Flint?

"She'll make a clever woman," says Mr. Bivins.

"I hope she may, Squire Bivins; I know it, Squire" (a strong thump upon the table here); "I shall guard her, sir; I shall watch her; she shall have everything heart can desire."

Poor Harry Flint, struggling for your own support, and that little one which Heaven has cast upon your kind keeping, what can you offer of worldly goods? What fancies could you indulge? And the poor fellow tries hard to choke his sentiment with philosophy. Could he be ungenerous enough to tie that sweet creature to his uncertain fortunes? But the trial is over now. The hope that burned in him is gone out.

Yet, so strange is the lithe heart of youth, a new one takes its place. Tied no longer to that little corner of country, he will brave the world, and win a fortune; and if no dearer recipient of his bounty can be found, he will lavish it upon the tender sister, who is growing every day in beauty and in grace.

There is a change in Harry Flint when he goes

home that day. Not less fondly does he clasp little Bessie; and stroking the hair from her forehead, he repeats his kisses oftener than ever before. Our loves are, after all, like rivers, which, if they be shut up here and there in their courses, will flow swift into side-channels, pushing always onward! With the fire and pride of youth upon him, Harry Flint decides to try his venture upon a broader field; and in a little time his arm and heart will struggle amid the whirl of a great city.

There is no prouder sight in this American world of ours than that of youth flinging off all the bondage of circumstance, trampling down, if need be, the memory of by-gone griefs, and measuring his fate, with a stout hand and heart, against the roar and vices of the world. He may be sure that singleness of purpose will bear him up, and earnestness of endeavor will bear him on, to accomplish just so much of work, and to win so much of renown, as his fullest capacities can grasp. Nothing lies in the way—thank God!—but the feebleness of individual effort. There are no old walls of privilege to batter down; there are no locks upon intellectual attainment that need a golden key. Strike out boldly, friend Harry; the world is wide; and although the memory of a love which might have been, may haunt your eventide hours, and make your affections droop, warm hearts are beating everywhere; and little blue-eyed Bessie, wearing the mother's face, and more and more the mother's figure, shall steal upon your remembrance, like a golden sun of April upon the skirts of winter.

Mr. Bodgers finishes his will. He does not, however, sign it. He is a calculating man: he will keep it by him until the next day; some new legacy may occur to him.

Squire Bivins, being, as he thinks, a shrewd man, argues from all this, that Mr. Bodgers is plainly intent upon marrying—not Kitty, but the Widow Fleming. He even ventures to hint in a sly way, looking very drolly over his spectacle bows, that "the widow is an uncommonly smart sort of a person."

Mr. Bodgers assents gravely.

Mr. Bivins, smoothing the curve of his wig behind, thinks "she would make a capital wife for the Squire."

Mr. Bodgers says, emphatically—"Fudge!"

If any widow ladies translate this expression into a reflection upon their worth and attractions, I shall simply say that it is a disingenuous construction.

Whatever may be thought of the Fudge, or its significance, Mr. Bodgers certainly did walk from the office of Mr. Bivins straight toward the home of Mrs. Fleming. The thought of marrying her, however, I do not think once occurred to him. Middle-aged men, who have tender recollections of their own, of lost ones, are not apt to fall in love with middle-aged widows; at least such is not my own experience.

Mr. Bodgers was anxious to have the last news of Kitty: and he threw himself, quite at ease, into an old arm-chair; and having placed his hat beside him, in the methodic way that belongs to him, and thrown his yellow bandanna within it, he listens to Mrs. Fleming, as she reads to him a bit, here and there, from the last letter of Kitty.

Meantime, Mr. Bodgers looks earnestly into the fire, musing, in a philosophic vein:—how it was once with him, and how it is once with us all: cheer, and joy, and sadness; and then, perhaps, decay and blight, and only glimpses of cheer; and at length, desolation, and the end.

"I am well, and happy," writes Kitty; "indeed, I am only not happy when I think of the distance that lies between us. You will smile because I make so much of so little distance. I am no great traveller, you know; and when I think of the strange things here—of all the noise, and the crowds, and the new faces, and the thronged streets—

and then, a little while after, think of the dear, quiet home I have left, and the good friends, and the old parlor, with its sunny blaze upon the southern window, and the hyacinths shooting higher and higher in the parlor warmth, and of you, dear mother, sitting there alone, it seems a very great way off!"

"My cousins are very kind to me."

Mr. Bodgers nods his head, as if he would say, "No wonder."

"Aunt Phœbe I do not see very often, nor Cousin Wilhelmina; although they talk very kindly, more kindly than the other cousins; but yet, I cannot help thinking, they are not so kind. They have a beautiful house; but I never feel at home there. Uncle Solomon is so grave and so important that there is no loving him, even if he were willing to be loved."

"Umph," says Mr. Bodgers.

"I have a gift for you, Mamma; a rich, warm shawl, which I am sure will keep you all the warmer, because your own Kitty has bought it for you. You must not think me extravagant; you know I told you that Uncle Truman had filled my purse for me. Is he not very kind?"

Mr. Bodgers takes occasion to look after his yellow bandanna. He likes to see that it is safe—that is all.

"You do not know how eagerly I am hoping for the time when I shall be at home with you once more. I like the city, and feel sure that I am gaining somewhat here; but it is not, after all, the old home, with the sunshine, and the flowers, and the walks, and you, dear Mamma!

"I shall be there when the birds come, and the garden is made again, and we will be *so* happy.

"God bless you, Mamma: and do not, and I am sure you will not, ever forget to love your own Kitty."

"POSTSCRIPT.—Give my love to Uncle Truman, and ask him if he is not coming to see us soon?"

"Very soon," thinks Uncle Truman.

"*Another Postscript.*—Pray what has become of Harry Flint and all the rest? Do write me. I love to hear about everybody. KITTY."

"Umph!" says Mr. Bodgers; "a beautiful letter, Mrs. Fleming."

And if Mr. Bodgers were more learned in those pretty deceptions which a young girl forces upon her own heart, he would not admire her second postscript, or stroll in so pleasant humor toward his lone home.

Not that Mr. Bodgers is in love with Kitty Fleming. Men of his age, they say, have outlived such weaknesses. Perhaps so. And yet Mr. Bodgers, with his forty-odd years upon his head, does feel from time to time a kind of spasmodic action of the heart ; a sort of restless inquisitive yearning ; an unsatisfied, eager longing, which he cures for the time being by calling up some such healthful, blooming, cheerful, earnest girl-face as that of little Kitty.

"Forty-five," muses Mr. Bodgers ; "it is not so very old. Many men marry later, and young girls at that. Thirty-five would be better : and Kitty—let me see—must be nineteen. Kitty is a sensible girl, very mature for her years ; a sweet girl is Kitty, very."

"Fudge ! nonsense !" muses Mr. Bodgers ; "what an old fool I am becoming !"

Thereupon Mr. Bodgers takes his will from his pocket, and reads it over, commending its provisions ; all, is not too much for Kitty. And in this mood he enters his lonely home. Very silent it is, with all its comforts. No little canary-singer on the wall welcomes him ; there are no dainty hands to care for such sweet songsters. The fire is burning cheerily, but it lightens no pleasant faces. The afternoon sun comes stealing into the western windows blithely; as blithely as twenty-odd years gone by; as blithely as it will do twenty years to come.

Mr. Bodgers sits down under the warm rays, and

tries hard to be cheerful. He runs over the outlines of his property ; he sums up his large estate ; but this gives no special cheer. He indulges in the recollection of some happy speculation ; yet he grows no gayer. He recalls the fairy movements of little Kitty as she moved about that very parlor, in attendance upon his poor, blind mother ; but even this does not make him cheerful.

He throws off his brown surtout, and strides across the room with a vigorous step ; and glances at the mirror ; and gives his hair a twist, and looks again, and half sighs. He is not growing cheerful, by any manner of means.

He feels the years creeping on him (as we all do), with their frailties and feebleness, and halting pulse, and sinking cheek. And memories brood in the twilight around the corners of his room, making him all the lonelier for these spectral visitants of his brain : harsh memories of losses and of deaths, of sickness and of sorrow; pleasant memories of smiles, and laughter, and rejoicings ; but all leaving him only quieter, soberer, lonelier !

What a sunbeam in the old home would not Kitty make, if her pleasant face was only beaming there with half the gladness that he has seen upon it ; if her pleasant voice was witching his ear, or she, leaning quietly upon his shoulder, growing sad with his sadness; looking as he looks upon the changing fire-play; imaging unconsciously his brightest thought in her own sweet, placid face!

Ah, Truman Bodgers, Truman Bodgers! if——

XIII.

Aunt Solomon Gains Ground.

"More qualifications are required to become a great fortune than even to make one; and there are several pretty persons about town ten times more ridiculous upon the very account of a good estate than they possibly could have been with the want of it."

Steele.

MRS. SOLOMON FUDGE has attempted to make her way in New York society, and her way she is going to make. What she undertakes to do—and I quote her own words—she is in the habit of doing. That is her style; and a very effective style it is.

She is eminently a "strong-minded" woman. If fortune had determined her lot at the head of an Orange county dairy, she would have grown up remarkably red in the face, strong in the elbows, tyrannic in her demeanor to milk-maids, and eminent in cheeses. As it is, the surplus energy of her character works off pleasantly in furbelows, coach-driving, opera-going, and assiduous cultivation of respectably-connected young men.

She is gratified with evidence of very perceptible gain in her advances : I see it in her air ; I see it in her treatment of the whimsical Mr. Bodgers ; I see it, I am sorry to say, in her comparatively negligent treatment of myself. The time was when my youthful air, jaunty toilet, and hotel habitude, rendered my visits impressive and desirable. My aunt delighted in my society ; she gained from me, in a circuitous way, a great deal of information as to what was doing in polite circles ; and a great many valuable hints in regard to the city education of Washington and Wilhelmina. That time is gone by. I feel myself growing, week by week, of less consideration.

Mrs. Fudge has achieved, through the indirect and unwitting action of Mr. Bodgers, an acquaintance with that elegant young man, Mr. Quid. A little blight seems to hang upon his father's business character ; in virtue of which, it is thought, the son is possessed of a large supply of ready money. As for the mother, there is little said or known about her ; she lived and died in Paris, and was very probably connected with a princely family—perhaps that of the Great Mogul himself.

Through Mr. Quid, Mrs. Fudge contrives an acquaintance with young Spindle ; who, being eminently fashionable, and having formed, as rumor reports, very distinguished acquaintances abroad, is quite a feather in the Fudge connection. I may take occasion to remark here, that a young man of ambitious social tendencies can hardly play a better card than by forcing his way—whether by presumption or strategy—into the houses of British gentlemen of reputation. Not a few individuals have come to my knowledge who are now trading largely and successfully upon this capital alone. The matter exposes us, it is true, to the occasional querulous observations of such grumblers as Mr. Carlyle ; but, on the other hand, it supplies our choicer circles with numerous young men of sharp shirt-collars and intense interest. For my own part, I must confess that I always feel a little doubtful of those social attractions which never seem to be appreciated except they make their appearance over seas and out of sight. One of the best ways in the world for a man to be a gentleman, is to be a gentleman—at home.

Mrs. Fudge has educated, and is educating, Wilhelmina—to be married. It is a common aim of city education ; perhaps the very commonest. Properly pursued, it is a worthy aim ; grateful to parents, and especially grateful to daughters. I am inclined to think, however, that it should not be the only aim of life, even with young ladies. Very many would probably disagree with me. Mrs. Fudge, in her secret heart, I am confident would do so. Wilhelmina would do the same.

It is my opinion that she does justice to her education, and that a prospective husband, rich, elegant, of good position and yielding manners, is rarely out of her thoughts or foreign to her plans. I am confident that she dwells upon the topic, and shows a power and fertility of imagination in that direction which would be utterly incomprehensible, except by young ladies similarly educated. I should not wonder if she had espoused, in fancy, a dozen or more of the most distinguished-looking young men at present upon the stage of city life.

It would be interesting, indeed, to compute what proportion of the young ladies' private talk, of the city or of watering-places, bears relation, either remotely or directly, to husbands for themselves, or to husbands for some one else. It would be interesting to know what variety and fertility of discussion illustrates those moral, mental, and physical qualities which go to make up *une bonne partie.* I have sometimes thought of taking up the matter myself, and of executing a treatise upon the subject: and what with my intimacy with Aunt Solomon and Wilhelmina, to say nothing of Bridget, Jemima, and the like, I am confident I could achieve a very popular work.

Miss Wilhelmina, like most girls of eighteen or nineteen, has her instinctive likings, and very romantic ones at that. But under cautious motherly guidance, they have not as yet cropped out very luxuriantly. I suspect she was in love with her music-master—the delightful pale Pole already alluded to. And had Monsieur Hanstihizy been John Brown, of the firm of Witless and Brown, wealthy hide-dealers, and strong upon 'change, the affection would have been encouraged, doubtless ; and perhaps reciprocated.

I am gratified by the confidence which Miss Wilhelmina reposes in me. She communicates with me very freely ; especially in reference to the remarks dropped in her hearing by her gentlemen admirers. I am inclined to think that she likes to ascertain, in a careless way, my interpretation of their inuendoes, though she does not say this. It is certain that she listens very kindly and keenly to any gratuitous explanations of mine. Generally, however, she had surmised "as much herself." She is "by no means disposed to count men in earnest—

not she. She has seen too much of society for that, she hopes."

Mrs. Fudge, being a keen observer, is a reasonably good tactician; her tactics, however, are rather *brusque;* and I have a fear that she may injure Wilhelmina's prospects in consequence.

The real state of Mrs. Fudge's feelings I take to be this; indeed, in confidential moments I think she may possibly express herself to her daughter in this way:

"Wilhe, dear, you are my only daughter, and I naturally take great pride in your success. You are now getting to an age at which you may reasonably hope to create some remark. Your father's position is a good one in the moneyed world, and also to some extent in the political. You will not forget, my dear, that your father was for some time mayor.

"Washington I hope brilliant things from on his return from Paris. He was always inclined to dancing, and he has a distinguished figure.

"Do not be in haste to be married, my dear; there is no greater mistake a young girl can make. You have advantages—great advantages. It is highly proper that you should use them. Try and be conciliating, Wilhe. Young Mr. Quid is an interesting person, besides being fashionable. I hear that he is wealthy, and I would be cautious about offending him seriously. At the same time, a little piquant quarrel is often very serviceable, and gives you occasion to appear very amiable. You should treat Tommy Spindle with great consideration: he is of a distinguished family, and you will find an intimacy with him—I might almost say, if I approved of such things, a flirtation—very serviceable.

"Your cousin Tony (the reader will spare my blushes) I beg you to humor: he is past the age when you need have any fear of an association of your name with his; and there being a remote cousinship, I think you might banter him very familiarly. With all his conceit, he has really seen a good deal of society; and though I would by no means recommend direct questioning, yet you may pick up a good deal of instruction from him about society, without his once suspecting your design.

"Your cousin Kitty you should treat kindly. It is not necessary to be familiar. She is a poor girl, and, as you must see, quite countrified. She seems an amiable, sprightly creature, and with your advantages, Wilhe, of position and of wealth, would very likely have been a belle. I think young Spindle has met her, and is pleased with her. You should take occasion to speak kindly of her—especially of her naïve country manner.

"Bridget and Jemima are very good girls in their way, and we must invite them here some day; perhaps during Lent. But I beg you would keep yourself on your guard, and don't show a familiarity upon which they can at all presume."

As for my uncle Solomon, I suspect he has never been very much interested in the fashionable *ménage* of my aunt. It humors him to find Wilhe admired; it would humor him more to see her married to the son of a fat broker, of large expectations. He regards everything about the town, and in the world generally, as ephemeral and sentimental, which does not have reference to stocks or good position in the moneyed circles. He delights in the respect shown him by quite a horde of bank-clerks; he admires their reverence; he is gratified by it. He has the highest regard for such benefactors of their race as the Rothschilds, Barings, and the late Mr. Astor.

He likes to see his name in the papers; and if he could at breakfast read the announcement that "our eminent merchant, Mr. Solomon Fudge, late mayor, has, we understand, entered into partnership with the house of Barings, and will henceforth occupy himself with the supervision of their American business," he would be ready to die at dinner, and leave my aunt a widow. I am confident of this.

The last Fudge ball was reckoned, I am proud to say, one of the crowning triumphs of the season. In some of the details of ceremonial my advice was deemed essential. I feel justified in saying that it was fashionably attended. Mrs. Fudge having made interest with one or two old belles of a tractable disposition, by virtue of a shower of opera-tickets and such like attentions, had the pleasure of greeting a great many desirable people for the first time. The Spindle girls, after long discussion, had consented to honor madame : it was remembered that Mr. Fudge had been mayor; that the daughter was *bien élevée;* and that Washington, on his return from Paris, might turn out—who could tell?—something desirable.

Mrs. Fudge was earnest in her receptions, and very red in the face : at best it is hot work, but with my aunt Solomon's intensity of manner, I am sure it must have been frightful.

Desirable young men were even more abundant than the same quality of ladies. They are, I observe, by far less fastidious in their socialities than the gentler sex : besides which, the suppers on such occasions are specially bounteous, and fresh flirtations offer with those bouncing parvenues, who are very apt to put on a little boldness of manner and familiarity of approach, to cover, perhaps, a certain lack of the habit of society.

A certain Count Salle, with eye-glass and white waistcoat, set off with crimson edging, was absolutely ravishing. His devotion to Miss Wilhelmina was unbounded ; and I have my suspicions that he uprooted many of those tender feelings which my cousin had previously entertained for young men generally, and Mr. Quid in special. It was delightful to witness the matronly pride with which my indulgent aunt regarded this new and brilliant conquest. It is quite impossible to picture the irradiation of her face : only the presence of Washington to bewitch the three Misses Spindle—a feat he would undoubtedly have accomplished—was needed to complete her triumph.

I cannot say that any unusual or important incident occurred. At a New York party they do not ordinarily occur. The loss of a new hat, or even of sobriety itself, is not to be spoken of. The good humor and social *bonhommie* of the old-fashioned, quiet gathering is gone from our day. And the modern jam seems to me to bear about the same relation to a fairly-filled room of genial people, who are not shy of each other, that a fashionable dinner-party—where you have to gauge your conversation by the card upon your neighbor's plate—bears to the old sort of cozy companionship of four good fellows over a generous joint and a pot-bellied little decanter of South-side wine.

Of course my aunt thought differently; and so thought Wilhelmina; and Uncle Solomon yielded to it, as one of the disagreeable necessities of what Mrs. Fudge calls their "growing position." I have heard of other husbands who have yielded in the same way, and for the same reasons.

I said that no incident occurred; I mistake. An incident did occur. It was verging toward the middle of the night. Madame was fully satisfied that Wilhelmina had acquitted herself bewitchingly, and had succeeded in captivating that elegant gentleman, the French Count. She had gratulated herself on having won such honor in the eyes of the Pendletons as would entitle her to a respectful bow from their carriage ever after; she felt sure of this. She had even ventured across the room, to drop a few encouraging words to that neglected lady, the elder Miss Spindle, when she was startled by the abrupt entrance of a stout, middle-aged gentleman, with his arm swung in a yellow bandanna, and accompanied by a gentle, timid girl in white muslin, with only a simple coral necklace, by way of ornament.

The parties were Mr. Bodgers, and our little friend Kitty. The old gentleman greeted "Cousin Phœbe" in the most friendly manner imaginable; assuring her that he never saw her looking "smarter"—that she was "plump as a partridge;" which indeed she was, and a very fat partridge at that.

The Misses Spindle tittered immoderately; and Mrs. Pinkerton looked as if she thought the presence of such a kindly-spoken old gentleman, was a personal affront.

As for my aunt Phœbe, her color became frightful;—most of all when the old gentleman, in excess of good-feeling, or of mischief-loving, patted her, with his sound arm, upon the shoulder.

Never was a bit of kindness so ungratefully received in the world. And Mrs. Solomon would, I am sure, have given half the wax-lights in the room, to be rid of the old gentleman and his pretty *protégée.*

Miss Kitty possessed that charming coyness of manner which attracts in the town assemblages, not less for its intrinsic beauty than for its exceeding rarity. Indeed, I suspect that she created a diversion among the besiegers of my cousin Wilhelmina, which may possibly work unexpected consequences. And she did this all the more effectively (let me say, for the benefit of those concerned) because she did it quite unconsciously.

Mr. Spindle, who had once breakfasted in company with a baronet, and accomplished many similar social feats, appeared to be quite charmed with the native graces of Kitty; and paid her a degree of attention that proved a very successful offset to the coquetries of Wilhelmina with the Count. For there is something, after all, in a fair and honest girlish brow, though it be not set off with the arts and the smirks of the town education, which steals its way to the inner places of even a bad man's heart, and which kindles in him a little wishfulness of better things than belong to the high-road of fashion.

How it happened that Mr. Bodgers and Miss Kitty should be in such place at such time, and how my little cousin Kitty sustained herself under the exuberant addresses of Mr. Quid, I must take another chapter to tell.

——Not, however, before I go back to follow the Parisian advances of my excellent male cousin, George Washington Fudge, whom I left amid all the delightful experiences of an intrigue with the elegant Miss Jenkins.

XIV.

An Intrigue by Wash. Fudge.

"He that will undergo
To make a judgment of a woman's beauty,
And see through all her plasterings and paintings,
Had need of Lynceus' eyes, and with more ease
May look, like him, through rime mud walls, than make
A true discovery of her." MASSINGER.

MASTER FUDGE had discovered, if I remember rightly, that the *incognita* of the masked ball could be none other than his old companion of shipboard, Miss Jenkins. He exulted, if I remember, in the discovery. It certainly was amusing. He felt that he was gaining ground. He enioyed his mirror excessively. Paris observation had not been in vain. He had grown killing. I think, in view of the circumstances, I might be allowed to express a certain degree of pity for Miss Jenkins.

Washington Fudge, however, did no such thing —not he; the inexorable, the complacent, the ravishing, the elegant, the merciless Wash. Fudge! It is really painful to think what a hecatomb of young ladies are annually offered up, sacrificed, burnt, absolutely consumed, in the devotional fires which such young men inspire. Their fearful cruelties they wear like honors, and prey ferociously, summer after summer, upon poor, weak, harmless, unresisting women. It is my opinion that they should be restrained, caged, bound with pink ribbons, their moustaches shaven—anything, in short, to prevent the sad ravages which they are committing in the great world of hearts! It is further my opinion that such restraint or imprisonment would not be felt, except by the parties themselves.

Now Mr. Fudge was growing riotous one fine morning over this strange and unexpected conquest of his, when he was agreeably startled by the receipt of still another perfumed billet from the same hand as before, full of pretty praises of his gallantry and his finesse of spirit; and offering, in courtly terms, the privilege of another interview; always, however, under the same precaution of the mask and secresy.

Such an intrigue, so mysterious, so rich, and

offering such staple for talk among the boys at home, was vastly gratifying to Mr. Fudge. The notes he guarded as trophies, and the second adventure proved even more mystifying than the first. Miss Jenkins was certainly most adroit in her manœuvres. Wash. Fudge ventured to hint, in a timid manner, the possible identity of his domino with a certain fair young lady of Atlantic experience, etc.

To all which inuendoes the domino replied by very significant shrug and deft management of her fan; intended, perhaps, to allay suspicion; but in this particular instance tending to confirm it to a very remarkable degree. I shall enter no defence of the inhumane manner in which my cousin Wash. Fudge exulted in his conquest over the heart of Miss Jenkins.

He determines to call upon that young lady, and to intimate in his graceful manner that "the secret was out"—that he felt sensible of the honor conferred, etc. His professor, who seems well posted in the *morale* of these things, highly approves the procedure. He warns him, however, that a lady in such a position will naturally avail herself of a thousand playful *équivoques*.

I beg leave, then, to attend Wash. Fudge as he makes his way, upon a cheerful afternoon, after his usual two-o'clock bottle of *vieux Macon*, to the second floor of a substantial hotel in the Rue Rivoli. A little tremor did very possibly overtake him as he ascended the waxed stairway, and listened to the distant tinkling of the bell, *au seconde*. It is not the easiest matter in the world, after all, to approach a pretty lady, who has made some coy advances. Ladies, I have remarked, bear that sort of face-to-face encounter much better than the men—especially such very young men as my cousin Wash. Fudge.

Howbeit, with the *vieux Macon* tingling pleasantly in his brain, and the memory of his last interview diffusing an agreeable warmth over his system, Mr. Fudge awaited, in one of those charming little salons which overlook the garden of the Tuileries, the appearance of his adventurous entertainer.

That she should take a little time to prepare herself for the ordeal was a circumstance which seemed to Mr. Fudge at once highly proper and natural.

Miss Jenkins is looking well—very well. Those Paris modistes do somehow give a very telling tournure even to the frailest of American beauties. Her face and eye, however, were all her own.

Mr. Fudge was delighted to meet Miss Jenkins—"quite."

Miss Jenkins manifests a very gracious surprise.

Mr. Fudge hopes that she is well—"indeed, he need not ask; the fatigues of Paris life do not seem to overcome her."

"Not at all."

"Yet the balls are rather serious."

"You find them so, Mr. Fudge?"

"Ah, not fatiguing, by no means, *au contraire;* but what do you think, Miss Jenkins, of three o'clock in the morning, in close domino and cruel mask."——

"Indeed, I am not familiar with such experience, Mr. Fudge."

"Not familiar? (a playful *équivoque,* thinks Mr. Fudge); and perhaps Miss Jenkins has *never* ventured to amuse herself in this way," with a leer, that somewhat surprises our American lady.

"You are quite right, sir."

"Ah, quite right, I dare say, Miss Jenkins (another playful *équivoque*): and do you fancy, Miss Jenkins, that those rich eyes could be mistaken, or that delicate hand?" (Mr. Fudge proposes to take it.)

"Sir!"

"Seriously now, Miss Jenkins," and Mr. Fudge throws a little plaintive honesty into his tones, "had I not the pleasure of a delightful promenade at the masked ball with a most graceful and piquant lady, and that lady—could it—could it, Miss Jenkins, be any other than yourself?"

"What does this mean, sir? Do you imagine I could so far forget myself?"

"Piquant as ever!"

"But, sir"——

"Oh, it's all right, Miss Jenkins; only a little continuation of the play."

"You are impertinent, sir."

"Ah, Miss Jenkins, Miss Jenkins (with very tender plaintiveness), and with these sweet notes (taking them from his pocket) in such a dear little, ladylike hand; surely you will not be so cruel."

"Sir, are you aware to whom you are talking?"

"Perfectly (the *vieux Macon* is in the poor young man's head); to the divine Miss Jenkins, the *domino qui domine touts cœurs!*"

"Sir, you are insufferable!" and Miss Jenkins, rising, rings the bell, angrily.

"Marie, you will show this gentleman the door."

It was a conjuncture my cousin Wash. had not anticipated—a very disagreeable conjuncture. He, however, summons resolution to kiss his hand to the "divine" Miss Jenkins, and passes out. His embarrassment is not relieved by the reception, a few hours after, of the following rather disagreeable note from his late fellow-passenger, Mr. Jenkins:

"Mr. Fudge will much consult his own advantage in abstaining from the imposition of any more of his drunken and impertinent fooleries upon the society of my daughter. THOMAS JENKINS."

The truth is, Mr. Jenkins was a man who, having married a fortune, had come to Paris to escape, as he said, American vulgarity; and to win by his money a consideration in the old world, which his small force of character would never give him in the new.

He was not inclined to favor the extraordinary advances of our cousin Wash. His letter was not complimentary; young Fudge and the old professor, who was in some measure a confidant of advances, were agreed upon this point.

Another happy adventure, however, of the opera-house ball restored the tone of Mr. Fudge's complacency; but what was his extraordinary surprise, to find that his charming *incognita* was perfectly informed of his interview with Miss Jenkins, and rallied him not a little, in her piquant way, and with the most voluble fore-finger in the world, upon his "drunken impertinences!"

Paris is surely a very strange place; and what

with blind doors in the wainscots, and hangings, and Napoleon's secret police, there was great food for the young and playful imagination of Mr. Fudge, junior.

Our hero was growing confused; a fact which, under the circumstances, will hardly appear unnatural. What might have been the result of this confusion, if unrelieved, it would be hard to say. He however found relief. In answer to the urgent solicitations pressed by him upon an evening at the ball, it was his good fortune to receive one of the most gracious little notes in the world—always written in the same delicate hand—inviting him, in the name of the Comtesse de Guerlin, to a "*petite soirée*, at No. 10, Rue de Helder."

A Countess!—happy Washington Fudge! thrice happy Mrs. Solomon Fudge! Who could have imagined that the weak-limbed son of the plethoric Solomon, that the late incumbent of a college-bench at Columbia, and the cherished son of Mrs. Phœbe Fudge (late Bodgers), should have won such brilliant conquest of a scion of the noble stock of Europe?

Yet it is true. He is there, at length, at the goal of his hopes; in the presence of a blooming dowager, who may have been forty, but better preserved than most American ladies of seven-and-twenty; and possessing that airiness of manner, and delicacy of figure which, joined to a fair skin, keen black eye, and glossy ringlets, were calculated to weigh upon the heart of our susceptible cousin Wash. like the graces of seventeen. I doubt if he even now admits that her years had run to four-and-twenty.

There was an elderly gentleman present, in white hair and white moustache, and in half-military dress, who received Mr. Fudge in quite a stately way: perhaps he was the father of the Countess; perhaps he was a count himself, or something of that sort; who knew?

But here I shall allow Washington to describe matters for himself. I shall quote from a letter with which I have been favored by one of his young friends at Bassford's. Nothing is altered, except the spelling. I observe that young persons familiar with French are apt to spell English badly.

"You should have seen the apartments," he says, "the neatest, genteelest thing you can possibly imagine, with or-molu, and *chefs-d'œuvre*, and all that: beside the delicatest statuettes. There was an old gentleman present, with white moustache, very distinguished-looking—might have been her uncle.

"She hinted to me, as I came in, by a whisper, that perhaps I remembered the interviews of the masked ball?

"'*Mais oui,*' says I, '*Madame.*'

"'*Eh bien*—not a word of it,' said she, and glanced at the old gentleman in the corner.

"'Enough said,' thinks I. Ain't I a lucky dog, Fred?

"She is uncommonly pretty; and these French women have such an artless, taking way with them! She presented me as a young English friend—ha, English! good, isn't it?—and highly recommended, *d'une famille distinguée*—Fudge. I think the old lady would prick up her ears at that!

"There was a Marchioness Somebody came in, in the course of the evening; a splendid-looking woman, but not equal to *ma belle.* There were two or three distinguished-looking men—officers of the government, I thought; and we had a little *écarté* together. I won some forty or fifty francs; didn't like to take it exactly, but they insisted. They are stylish, and no mistake.

"Since the first evening, I have been there frequently; and taken a drive or two in the Countess's *coupé* out to the Bois de Boulogne. Of course I have made her some magnificent presents; and, egad, I believe the old gentleman in the white moustache begins to be afraid that the Countess is a little tender my way!

"We play a little every evening; sometimes the luck runs rather against me; in fact, I am a little ashamed to be always winning in such company. The other evening I was in for seven hundred francs. But the Countess insisted on my not paying down, as I would be sure to win again.

"And faith, so I did; but the night after was down again to the tune of one thousand. However, I fancy it will all come out about even.

"I have tried to find how the Countess knew so much about me and my affairs; but she always staves it off in the prettiest way in the world. She has got an idea, too, that I am confoundedly rich. I tell her it isn't so; at which she makes up the prettiest and most coquettish face you can imagine.

"I met on her stairs the other day my old professor. It struck me, at first, that perhaps he knew her, and had "peached" on me. But it can't be. Do you think it can?

"She tells me I speak too well to need a professor any more; and she has the delicatest way of saying, '*Mon cher, tu parles bien Français; pas tout à fait comme Parisien, mais—si gracieusement!*'

"Colonel Duprez is the name of the distinguished-looking gentleman I meet there. He plays devilish well at *écarté*—most full of anecdote; he must have suffered immensely in his day—but not at cards.

"P. S. I have just come in from the Rue de Helder. It's about two A. M., and I am nervous. To tell the truth, I am in for seven or eight thousand francs. The Countess bet on my hand, and I thought myself safe. She don't seem to mind the loss at all.

"I am afraid the governor will get wind of the matter. If you happen up at the house, do talk to the old lady about the immense expense of living in Paris; at least, in genteel society.

"I may work it off to-morrow. But the Colonel has got an I. O. U. from me. My bankers are about dry, and I shall have to come down for a cool three thousand. I hope that the Dauphin is doing a confounded round business, and the old man in humor.

"Remember me to the boys."

XV.

WITH NOT MUCH IN IT.

"THE heart is a small thing, but desireth great matters. It is not sufficient for a kite's dinner, yet the whole world is not sufficient for it."

HUGO.

IT is strange that a man living so comfortably as Mr. Bodgers should not have been satisfied. Why, pray, does he not take the world easy? And you, my dear sir, or madam, turned of forty, with enough of money and no family; with a house and old silver; with a horse and gig, and may be, a good pew in the church; why on earth are *you* not satisfied?

What business have you to be troubled about your cook, or your carpenter, or your broker, or your life past, or your life to come? Haven't you it all nearly in your own way? Are you not, like

8*

an old simpleton, quarrelling with yourself all the while, merely because you haven't any little family about you to tease you, and worry you, and so give you some sensible reason for being annoyed?

Well, Mr. Bodgers was fidgety. The fire vexed him: it wouldn't burn as he wished. The sunshine vexed him: it was so warm, and so grateful, and so cheap, and none but he in the great parlor. His coat vexed him; and the people of the town vexed him: most of all, it vexed him to see his next-door neighbor (who was only a carpenter) fondling his little daughter. What business has a man to be enjoying himself in this way, and to be eternally taunting us with our condition? Mr. Bodgers took snuff for relief.

And having taken snuff, he thinks of his Will, and of Kitty; and glancing out of the window again, he thinks he will go to town and see how little Kit is getting on.

And being in town, and learning that cousin Phœbe was to give a party, to which the Misses Fudge, with Kitty, had been invited (at a very late hour), he insists in his usual way, that Kit should go and have a sight of the world. Partly, no doubt, he was anxious to tease the old lady by his presence, and partly to enjoy the admiration he felt sure would belong to his little country friend.

"A fig for dress!" said Mr. Bodgers. And so (although between the discussions of Jemima and Bridget, about the purple dress and the pink one, and the salmon-color with gimp trimmings, Kitty came near having no chance to dress at all), it was arranged that our little country cousin should wear a simple white muslin. And very prettily she looked in it; so prettily that the spinster cousins insisted upon half a dozen kisses each, much to the admiration of the fond old Mr. Bodgers; and to his vexation too.

I think the coral necklace, the only ornament she wore, rather added to the effect of Kitty's complexion; it was certainly the most charming color I ever saw. Mrs. Bright, who had no daughters, and was a brunette, made the same remark. "Perfectly irresistible," said I—"for a blonde."

Mrs. Bright bowed, and begged me to join her party for the ninth. (Mrs. Fudge's ball was on the sixth of the month.)

Kitty enjoyed it all very much, as a sensible young lady from the country on her first visit ought to do. For she was made of flesh and blood like the rest of us, and admired the brilliant dresses, and the music, and the dancing; and in short, was quite intoxicated with it all.

"Who is she?" said a great many, looking

through their quizzing-glasses. And Kitty, whose ears were sharp, heard them say it ; and her heart, which was not altogether a flint one, bounded under the little white bodice, in a way that sent the blood, in a very lively manner, over her face.

"And how pretty !" said other ladies (old ladies mostly) ; and Kitty heard that too, and received it, as young ladies always do, in a most cordial and grateful manner. For she was no saint. I do not think a saint would make a sensation in our world, or be greatly admired in New York.

Strange as it may seem, Kitty enjoyed the attentions of such elegant young gentlemen as Mr. Quid and Mr. Spindle ; so unlike as they proved to the monotonous chamber-talks of her spinster cousins. And beside, there belonged to them such piquancy of chat, and such admirable watchfulness of her humor (bless her guileless innocence !) and such playful, good-tempered, sportive sallies about this old lady's head-dress, or that one's blue and yellow brocade !

Uncle Truman, with his slung arm, wandering here and there, provoking smiles, that reddened more and more the rich color of my aunt Solomon, kept his eye ever upon the flitting figure in white muslin, and upon the coral necklace. Indeed, I suspect it was only to watch that little figure that he had found his way up to town ; and I more than suspect that all the home vexations which so preyed on him, would have found very great relief if he could only have wandered, as in past years he was used to wander, into Mrs. Fleming's cottage, and be greeted with one of Kitty's kisses.

Where our benefits and favors go, we like to go ourselves : and having lavished more than he ever lavished elsewhere upon Kitty Fleming, it was natural enough that he should love to watch her. But in the face of young Mr. Quid there was something that greatly disturbed Mr. Bodgers; and only the more because Kitty seemed ever so intent upon what he whispered in her ear. It was strange enough that the old man should be so jealous of a boy, and of a boy he must have seen and despised ; yet a boy, after all, who, when he has Mr. Bodgers' years, and his gravity, will not look unlike our uncle Truman himself.

How can it be ?

And when, after it is over, Mr. Bodgers, with Kitty leaning on his arm, strolls to her home, without any mention of a name (but with very much thought of the sleek-looking boy), he cautions her, in an old man's way, against the vanities and the pretensions of which the world is full.

She, all tremulous with the excitement which

such an evening will strew over the fancies of seventeen, listens kindly—how kindly! and smiles, and blushes to the moon, and feels her heart made twin with the love of the pleasantness gone by, and with grateful yearnings toward the old man (alas, that he is so old!) who watches over her, and guards her.

And Mr. Bodgers, listening to the trip of those young feet, as they twinkle between the heavy tread of his own, and looking down—oftener than he thinks—upon the little hand that clings so confidingly to his strong arm, provokes her gay prattle, and drinks it in, and admires, and smiles, and advises, with most curious and perplexed attention.

"Never mind wealth, or beautiful things, Kitty."

"Not mind them, Uncle Truman?"

"You shall have enough of them, Kit. I will see to that."

And the little hand closes over the stout arm—so kindly!

"Dresses, and jewels, and whatever you like, Kitty, if—only"—

"Well, Uncle Truman?"—

"—If only (he cannot say it)—if only—you will be always the same true-thoughted girl, and not have your heart turned topsy-turvy by these tricksy, good-for-nothing fellows."

"Oh no," says Kitty, wondering what he means all the while.

And when they are at the door, he says, with his hand in hers (which he hurts without meaning it), "Remember, Kitty!"

And she says, "Yes, Uncle Truman."

"I told you you should have whatever you wished, if you will only take it."

"You are so kind," says she.

"Good night, Kit: one kiss."

And he takes it. "Yes, she *shall*," says he to himself, "everything, *everything!*"

It is a starry and a moonlight night, and the old gentleman walks away, summing up the bounties and the luxuries he could and he will bestow upon her. There is a luxury, after all, in wealth, when we can give. But alas for us! it is almost always given too late.

Bridget is waiting to receive Kitty, who in the first burst of her excitement tells of all the kindness of Mr. Bodgers. (If he could only have heard her!)

"What a dear, good, awkward old gentleman," says Bridget. (If he could only have heard her!)

Afterward, upon a very restless pillow, Kitty runs over the scenes of the evening, and wonders (as young girls do wonder) if Mr. Quid, and the rest, were altogether so earnest as they seemed? And wonders if she herself is altogether so charming as they would make her believe? And wonders if this or that one, such elegant young fellows, will come to call upon her, as they have more than hinted? And wonders if she could love any one of them truly, as she only means to love? And wonders what Mr. Bodgers could mean by promising her "everything," in such a gentle manner? And then she blushes at the wonder, and says, "Oh no, absurd!" and composes herself for the night's rest.

But even now, her thoughts run swiftly to the old village, the evening's excitement deepening her affection only because the blood is flowing faster and freer (which she does not know), and murmuring blessings upon that country home, and upon her mother, and all, she drops asleep with a smile; a smile that (if one could see it) is all the prettier, because it is lighted with a tear.

XVI.

An Unfortunate Casualty.

"If the captain and owners of the Henry Clay are not punished for the recklessness, which resulted in the burning of that vessel, then there is no justice in the land."—New York Editorial, 1852.

NEXT morning Mr. Bodgers sent to Kitty a pearl necklace, and very rich it was; far prettier than one that Wilhelmina had worn the night before.

"Cousin Phœbe, with all her airs, sha'n't turn up her nose at little Kitty," said the old gentleman; and with that he took an amiable pinch of snuff, and blew his nose quite loudly, and walked off in a grand way.

It vexed him not a little to think of young Quid. To be sure, he knew nothing bad of him except his look, and his parentage. Squire Bodgers was not the man to treat complacently such a person as Quid senior. To pay one's debts was a part of what he counted good character; and he professed no sort of regard for a man who robbed legally, and paid his dues with what he wickedly called a "damnable civility." He always felt a strong disposition to çane the sleek-looking Mr. Quid, whenever he caught sight of him picking his steps through the streets, with his gold-headed stick, and forestalling sneers with the most profound obsequiousness.

If he had only suspected—what I must confess I had suspected for a long time—that Quid's late wife, and the mother of the dashing lad, who showed such annoying attentions the evening before, was perhaps a blood relation of himself (although a woman of uncertain character), I think his disposition to cane the widower would have been much stronger than it was.

It is certain he would not have left his Will so long unsigned in the pigeon-hole of his desk.

However, Mr. Bodgers returned to Newtown, quarrelled (amiably) with the foreman of his tan-works, scolded his house-keeper, and indulged in a hundred of those bachelor vexations which are so natural to men of his age and condition; and finally, one bright morning (it was spring weather), stepped around to Mr. Bivins' office to execute his Will.

Mr. Bivins was out; but Harry Flint, who had not yet arranged the leave-taking, at which I have hinted—and who, I am bound to say, had grown somewhat sallow and melancholy—occupied the office.

Squire Bodgers, who always went straight to his mark, and entertained (honest man that he was) a considerable contempt for legal talk and forms, wished to sign a paper. Mr. Flint was as good a witness as Mr. Bivins: and although two might have been better than one, one was better than none.

"Give us a pen, Harry," said the Squire.

And the pen was brought; and the Squire, with a very tremulous hand (for his arm was still lame), wrote "Truman Bodgers."

"It is my Will," said he. "Witness it, Harry."

Harry witnessed it without a word; for he thought still of the marriage settlements, and wished (almost) that the excellent Mr. Truman was in the other world. And he noticed with his lawyer's eye that the Squire's lame arm had executed a signature without his usual flourish.

"Give us your hand, Harry," said the Squire. "They tell me you are off?"

"Off to-morrow, sir," said Harry, "for California."

"God bless me! so far?" said the Squire.

"Well, be honest; stick to work; you're young, Harry, very young."

I think Mr. Bodgers sighed, as he marched home.

Three days after, he set off for town. His village was three or four miles from the river, and he drove down leisurely, taking little notice of a road which he passed over so often, and which he would probably pass over a great many times again. The people who lived there, his neighbors, bade him good morning, and said to themselves carelessly, "So the Squire is going to town."

The widow Fleming saw him, and called after him to "give her love to Kitty."

"That I will," said the Squire, and chuckled, when he thought that he would give his own too.

"I wish I was a trifle younger," says Mr. Bodgers to himself.

"Young enough," says Duty, silently (as Duty always talks when she talks loudest), "young enough to do good."

Mr. Bodgers could not say nay, so he whipped on, and at the landing he took the fast boat. It is a sad American cure for neglected duty, or for lagging charity, to get over the ground, or the water, fast. When we feel the spur of conscience, we stick the spur in our horse, and the glow of haste we take for the flush of fulfilment. In our hurry and scurry, the nerves grow dead; when the inner monitor asks what victories we have won, we point only to the wide space we have gone over. But there is coming a time to us all, when the distance that a life has made good will be measured, not by miles or by hundreds of them, but by the worthiness of deeds.

"Fudge!" you say. And the word brings me back to my story.

Mr. Bodgers took the Eclipse, being a faster boat than the Rapid. Yet the Rapid had made good time that day, and the boats were nearly abreast at the dock.

"We shall beat her twenty minutes into New York," said the captain, looking at his watch; and he went below to the fire-room.

Mr. Bodgers, although a cautious man (we are all cautious in our way), regarded the race with considerable interest. It was hinted, indeed, by some timid people, that there might be danger, and that it was "an abominable risk;" but nobody, save some few nervous ladies, were disturbed by such a hint as that. Once, indeed, there was a slight crash, which created some uneasiness; but it proved to be only the result of a playful manœuvre on the part of the pilot, who had dexterously run the bow of the Eclipse into the guards of the other boat, crushing a few timbers, and exciting quite a laugh among the loungers on the forward deck.

Mr. Bodgers thought such management improper, and said as much to Mr. Blimmer, whom he accidentally found on board, and whom he had occasionally met at the house of the widow Fudge. Mr. Blimmer, however, smiled sagaciously, and remarked in his usual voluble tones, that "We are a go-ahead people, a great people, Mr. Bodgers: boating, railroading, telegraphing, towns springing up in a day; wonderful people, sir. We shall be in town, sir, by five; think of that, sir! Eighteen miles in the hour, sir, against tide!"

Mr. Blimmer had found it for his interest to take stock in the Eclipse, as proprietor of Blimmersville. His card, with a diagram of the place, was hanging in the captain's office. The clerk was instructed to ask strangers if they had visited the pretty town of Blimmersville; and the steward had entered upon his bill of fare, "Blimmersville pudding." It was a dear pudding.

Mr. Blimmer assured Mr. Bodgers that there were a "few remaining lots at Blimmersville, which offered a capital chance for speculation; highly eligible lots, purposely reserved for men of standing and influence."

"Lots which sold at five dollars the foot, are

now selling, Squire, at fifteen. We have a capital grocer in the place, and (what is rare) an honest one. There are but a very few inferior or unhealthy locations, as the physician assures us, upon the property. These we have kept in reserve for public uses, either a parsonage, or infant school, or something of that kind."

Mr. Bodgers took snuff—a strong pinch.

Mr. Blimmer drew out his chart. He designated the favorable "locations." "This was for the church—Gothic, with four spires, one at each corner, bell in the tower; arrangements nearly matured with a city clergyman, a man of genteel connections, and well calculated to give respectablity to the village."

The Eclipse gained upon the Rapid, much to the satisfaction of the company upon the forward deck, who gave vent to their satisfaction by a subdued cheer.

Mr. Blimmer proceeded with his details, to the evident annoyance of Mr. Bodgers. "What do you think of the matter, Squire?" says Mr. Blimmer, confidently.

"I think, Blimmer, that it's an infernal humbugging business, from the parsonage down, and I'll have nothing to do with the matter." And he tapped his snuff-box vigorously.

I think Mr. Blimmer would have resented this, in his voluble way, if some timid ladies, frightened by the increased speed and heat, and the unusual creaking of the boat, had not implored the gentlemen to intercede with the captain.

"Pho, pho!" said Mr. Blimmer; "staunch boat; good captain; all right."

Mr. Bodgers, however, to whom it seemed that the press of steam was unusual, walked forward to drop a word to the engineer.

"We know what we are about, old fellow," said the engineer.

Presently—it could hardly have been ten minutes later—they said, somebody cried out that the boat was on fire. And to be sure, a little black smoke was coming out from the door of the fire-room.

"Pho, pho!" said Mr. Blimmer, folding up his chart, "it's nothing at all."

But soon there was blaze, as well as smoke; and a few of the people rushed forward, very fortunately, as it proved. But the greater part were calling out for the captain, or trying to calm the women, who were now screaming with fright. Nobody, however, seemed to know where the captain was; even Mr. Blimmer thought it "quite extraordinary," and said "*they* would run her ashore directly."

Still the boat headed down the river, the Rapid being now far behind; the pilot and engineers probably not being greatly incommoded by the flames, which now swept through the pass-ways on either side of the engine.

Mr. Bodgers, not losing his coolness as yet, took Blimmer by the arm (and it shows how common danger levels all anger and strife), "Blimmer," said he, "this may be a bad business; I accuse nobody, though the captain ought to be hung, if a soul dies. I have got a valuable paper in my pocket; it is my last will and testament; I don't know if it is altogether in legal form—but it is what I wish; I shall hand it to you; if I get to shore, I can renew it; if not (and the old gentleman did not tremble), it will be safe with you." And he handed him his will.

Blimmer put it in his coat-pocket.

By this time—for the time counted by minutes now, and the alarm was general—the ladies were well-nigh in a state of frenzy, and the boat was headed to the shore. Even Blimmer was in a state of nervous inquietude. The flames crackled and roared loudly; and there were hoarse orders screamed out now and then from beyond the smoke; but nobody seemed to know who gave them, or what they were. Indeed, the cries of the women were so loud in the after-part of the vessel, that it was impossible almost to distinguish any words at all.

A few persons in the inner cabin were praying for God to save them. Very likely, they were those who never asked Him for anything before.

One or two men, driven by frenzy no doubt, had thrown themselves overboard, from the forward deck; and came drifting by swiftly; and floated far off behind, where the sun seemed to lie very warmly on the water; but except they were good swimmers, which, saving one, they were not, they went down.

A poor little fellow of ten years old, or thereabout, came to Mr. Bodgers, and took his arm beseechingly. "Will you save me, Sir?" said he, "for my father is not here."

"God save you, my boy!" said Mr. Bodgers; "for no one else can."

At this, the boy cried; and Mr. Bodgers led him aft, and lashed him as well as he could, for his lame arm (the boy remembers him well), to a settee, and dropped him overboard; and he was picked up by a skiff half an hour after.

While this was passing, the boat was gaining the land, though the flames were spreading; and soon, just as the people were rushing up the stairway upon the hurricane-deck, the boat drove upon the shore. The shock threw many off their feet, and into the water.

Those who were upon the forward-deck, the captain and pilot and engineers among them (who had taken great care to be in a safe place), jumped ashore.

But for those in the after-part of the vessel, the danger was not yet over. The stern was swinging out two hundred feet or more from the land, and the water had good depth—some twenty feet, or perhaps more than that. A little strip of the upper-deck still remained good, though those who passed over it were compelled to pass through a wall of smoke and flame. A few adventurous ones, Mr. Blimmer among them, crossed over, and threw themselves from the bow upon the shore ; or at the worst, into very shallow water.

The women with their light dresses could never venture upon that passage through the flame. Indeed, the deck, which was but fragile, was even now yielding, and swaying with the fires below. Mr. Bodgers went forward, to cross ; but had the failing bridge yielded with him, lame as he was, it would have brought an awful death. And even while he hesitated, what remained of the upper deck about the engine fell with a crash ; and the blinding smoke and cinders drove him back to the extreme after-part of the vessel.

The scene was very terrible around him. Some few upon the shore, who had struggled through the water, were shivering with cold, and beckoning to those on board which way they had best go. And four or five noble fellows (among them a man who was honored before, and who is doubly honored now*) were struggling to save the helpless females, who, driven by the flames, dropped themselves into the river.

And those who had thrown themselves overboard were contending not only with the waves, but fiercely struggling with each other, like beasts. For fear had maddened them.

Mr. Bodgers turned his eyes from this. But there was no escaping the sight of Death : and one time or other, it will be the same for us all. Death was everywhere around him, crying to him—gurgling in his ears—staring at him with fixed eyes clutching him with cold fingers—dragging him under!

There was indeed one more chance left. If he could work his way around by that narrow edge of the guard, which projects about a hand's breath from the wheel-house, he might yet save himself.

* Mr. Downing.

For the flames had not fairly broken through the outer covering of the wheel ; or at most, only burst here and there through the cracks of the wood. Now and then, it is true, the wind drove the flame and smoke over the wheel, so that they reached the water ; but as it was the only chance, the old gentleman (praying, I doubt not, silently) ventured upon this narrow footway.

Mr. Blimmer, who had escaped, and retired for a while to the hill above the river, lest the boiler might explode, had come back now to the shore ; and espying Mr. Bodgers, shouted to him, very charitably, to come on, and gain the forward guards, and so leap to the land, as he had done.

The old gentleman had but one arm with which to cling, and the path was narrow ; beside, the flames, as I said, were shooting through the cracks of the wood, and becoming stronger every moment. But he went on bravely, his feet taking hold strongly of the little rib of timber, until he had half gone by the wheel ; but here, unfortunately, a sudden whiff of the wind brought over from the other side a great cloud of smoke and flame, which burned his hair and his hands ; and presently, so suffocated him, that he could keep his hold no longer ; and he dropped heavily into the river.

Even now there was a chance for him ; for the

land was only a hundred feet away, and he had been a strong swimmer in his time. But the weak arm crippled his strength; and one or two who were struggling in the water laid hold of him. A sloop's boat, which a noble fellow from the shore (I think he was a coachman) had manned, was going toward him, as he came up; and as he saw it coming, he struggled fiercely to shake off those who were holding upon him.

But before the boat came, his strength gave out; and with two persons clinging fast to him, in the sight of at least a hundred lookers-on, and under the warm spring sun (it was mid-afternoon of April), he went down—for ever!

"Pity!" said Mr. Blimmer.

As the evening wore on, and all the strugglers upon the wreck had fallen off, or were burned, they commenced dragging up the bodies from the river. Among others, they drew up the body of Mr. Bodgers, looking very ghastly, as the bodies of the drowned do always. No more fever, or vexation, or trouble of any sort, for the Squire! It was over.

(As for Mr. Blimmer, at ten o'clock—later by five hours than he had reckoned—he was in town; looking out for the interests of the owners, with the will of Mr. Bodgers in his pocket.)

And finally deep night fell; while the smoking

embers threw a glare along the shore, and lighted the faces of the drowned ones, lying high upon the beach. And the engine, upon the railway track near by, passed to and fro the livelong night; shrieking as it came near to the scene of the wreck; and bringing mourners.

And the moon stole up softly into the sky overhead; and the waves rose and fell with the changing tide, murmuring pleasantly, as they always do. But there were none to note these things; for Death, in company with the owners and the captain of the boat, had wrought a damnable work there!

We Americans live fast. It is all over now—the sorrow, and the crime.

XVII.

Squire Bodgers' Mourners.

A. Malum mihi videtur esse mors,
M. Tisne qui mortui sunt, an iis quibus moriendum est?
A. Utrisque.

Tusc. Quæst.

MR. BODGERS being dead, was mourned over. Most dead men become great favorites in society. It is an old story, but worth telling again in this connection, that nothing so much helps a man's reputation as—dying. I do not mean to commend it to my friends, lest I might be thought invidious and ungenerous. But yet I could lay my hands upon the shoulders of a great many capital fellows, whose hopes do certainly lie largest in that direction, and whose names will scarce be currently known, or on the lips of men for a week together, or, indeed, make any deep impression whatever, until they are cut in marble.

I do not mean, however, to say aught in crimination or to the discredit of Truman Bodgers. There were those who spoke in praise of him before, and with much good reason. But now, all Newtown repeated his eulogy. The old housekeeper, who could hardly have survived a week without some bickering with Truman, now put on as honest bombazine as ever grew tawny with wear, and said, with cambric to her eyes, "N'erry a man can fill the Squire's place."

And the wicked carpenter next door, who had often with his plane-iron whisked off a curling "D—n the old Square!" was now grave and thoughtful, and said that "few men, in the long run, were cleverer than Uncle Truman."

It is well and natural that these honors should gather about the dead. For what we do that is wrong and envious springs, for the most part, from the temptations and bedevilments that belong to our weak, frail bodies; and when once these are shaken off, and we have given our low-lived mortality the go-by, why, pray, should we not be credited the goodness which belongs to us, and which pertains, and will pertain evermore, to the ethereal part that is gone? The hand that smote us, and the tongue that belied us, and the eye that rebuked us, are dead: they cannot harm us any longer; nor any longer can they hurt him who held them, and who used them with earthy appetites. But the essence that shone in charity, and that kindled generous emotion, and that bowed the Man in silent worship of Deity and goodness, is living still (who knows how near?) and claims, by all human sympathy and all spirit-bonds, that we recognize it kindly.

The country clergyman improved the occasion in an elaborate sermon; commending the Christian worth and dignity of the old gentleman who had been nipped in the flower of his days; making Squire Bodgers, in short, only less eminent in the Christian graces and charity than the Napoleon of Mr. Abbott's history.

The newspapers, moreover—those hasty and impassioned eulogists of nearly all dead men—came boldly to the support of Mr. Bodgers' reputation. "We have again to record," said they, on the day succeeding the event, "one of those terrible calamities which succeed each other with frightful rapidity, and which call for something far more effective than a mere outburst of popular indignation. We trust that an example will at length be made of those who thus trifle wantonly with human life. There seem to us, in the present instance, no palliating circumstances. It is downright murder! The country demands a thorough investigation; and woe be to the reckless men who have thus put all considerations of humanity at defiance! Among the unfortunate victims, we are pained to notice the name of that highly respectable citizen of Newtown, Truman Bodgers, Esq., a most worthy and valuable member of society. His loss, to his family and the country, is irreparable. Again we say, shall the abettors of this infamous outrage be brought to justice? We pause for a reply."

Two days thereafter, the newspaper qualifies its remarks thus: "We understand, from a highly respectable gentleman who chanced to be on board at the time of the recent unfortunate casualty to the steamer Eclipse (we speak of Mr. Blimmer, of Blimmersville, whose advertisement may be found in another column), that the boat was making only its usual speed, and that the fire was one of those untoward accidents which no human foresight could possibly have prevented.

"Mr. Blimmer, having exerted himself in a noble manner on the occasion alluded to, is still suffering severely. We are informed through him, that Mr. Bodgers maintained his presence of mind to the last, and intrusted to him (Mr. Blimmer) sundry commissions of *considerable importance*. All the efforts of Mr. Blimmer to secure the safety of the old gentleman proved unavailing. We are happy to learn that Mr. Blimmer is in a fair way of recovering from the effect of his efforts in behalf of the unfortunate deceased.

"The paragraph characterizing the accident as murder, we beg to state, was written in the absence of the senior editor of this journal."

Mr. Blimmer, I have already remarked, is a wide-awake man, and part-proprietor of the steamer Eclipse. Mr. Blimmer was not familiar with the family of Mr. Bodgers. The paper in his hands might be of service—to himself. The hint thrown out in the "*Daily Beacon*" might induce some advances on the part of those interested. It seemed to him an ingenious way of conducting observations.

Mr. and Mrs. Solomon Fudge lamented the fate of Mr. Bodgers. And having recovered from their lamentation, discoursed in this way over the breakfast-table (Cousin Wilhe being in bed):

AUNT PHŒBE.—"Do you know, Soly, if Truman leaves a large estate?"

SOLOMON.—"Mrs. Phœbe, I think it must be large—quite large. The tan-works were profitable, very. He has a house or two in town, and considerable stock in our bank."

"And—Solomon—who—do you think, dear, are his heirs?"

"Nonsense, Phœbe! as if you didn't know that you and your sister Fleming were the nearest kin."

"But if he made a will, Soly?"

"Why, then, he did, my dear."

"La, Solomon! do you think he did make a will?"

"How should I know what to think?"

"There, now! so short, and I"—(handkerchief to face forbids distinct utterance).

"You can't alter the will, if it's made, can you, Phœbe?" says Uncle Solomon, relenting, and helping himself to a chicken-leg.

"No, Solomon; who said that I could?"

"Nobody."

"Well?"

"Well!"

"I hope he didn't, Solomon!"

"So do I, Phœbe, for your sake. You were never much a favorite with Truman."

"But he was so vulgar, Solomon."

"Ah, yes: Newtown man, Phœbe."

"There now, Solomon!"

The colloquy, however, finally ends in a promise on the part of Soly to visit Newtown and investigate matters.

Poor Kitty, with her best friend (saving only her mother) gone, is quieter and sadder. To her comes up the thought that she will not see again the kind old face that smiled on her ; that she will not hear again the kind voice that called down blessings on her ; that she would never welcome him, nor thank him, nor watch for him, nor meet him, ever again. Not once, as yet, comes up to her girlish thought, the reflection that both she and her mother had been almost dependent on his bounty ; nor once does the sense of any approaching want disturb her.

Is not the old homestead there, with her hopeful and welcoming mother, and the trees and sunshine, and God's providence over each and all ?

Our best mourners will prove, ten to one, the quietest ones ; and they whose tears will be better than masses performed for the gentle rest of our souls, will weep silently and out of sight.

But it did flash over Kitty, as she struggled with her grief, that she could stay no longer in the town, but must go back now to cheer the old homestead. And there were unpleasant thoughts joined to this leave-taking. The town grows strangely upon the affections of an impulsive, enthusiastic girl. Even its glitter and show flatter the eye, and woo the fancy strongly.

The Mr. Quids are not wholly despicable characters; far from it. They possess considerable tact and grace, and very great knowledge of dress. They are not unfrequently possessed of an easy and trifling amiability, such as finds an approach to the hearts of innocent girls.

It must be borne in mind, moreover, that the spinster cousins, the amiable Miss Jemima and Miss Bridget, were naturally enamored of young men in fashionable life, or of those who appeared to be in fashionable life; and it is not hard to believe that they should have transferred a portion of this enamored feeling into the bosom of pretty Kitty Fleming.

Nor, to tell truth, was Kitty very hard-hearted; she had a great deal of kindness in her composition—kindness to Uncle Solomon, kindness to me, kindness to young men in general. It was not altogether strange that she should feel kindly, then, toward a genteel young fellow who left bouquets at her door, such as would have utterly astonished the whole village of Newtown, and who, on one or two occasions had been instrumental, as she learned, in a very pretty serenade, which quite startled the spinster cousins, and which was the means of giving the grocer opposite an unusual view of Miss Bridget in her night-cap. I would not give a fig for a girl who has not her own share of pride; and Kitty had this; and she had felt it mortified sometimes by the bearing of Aunt Phœbe and Wilhelmina; and it was a good offset to this hurt feeling to have stolen away the most stylish of Cousin Wilhe's admirers.

Not that she would really harm Cousin Wilhe: but then there was a little gratification, when walking with Adolphus Quid, to meet with her showy cousin: and pray, what young girl of eighteen would not have felt the same?

Adolphus, too, was rather a pretty name. Not so bluff-sounding as Harry Flint, for instance; nor so honest-sounding, perhaps: but, as Bridget said, a "sweet name." In French, too, which she was studying, it rendered up gracefully into Adolphe, which agreed with that of a good many lively heroes of novels, with which girls studying French are apt to become acquainted.

Now I do not positively affirm that all this train of thinking passed through the mind of little Kitty, as she mourned and speculated upon her uncle's death: but association is a strange thing, and sets our imagination gadding often in strange quarters, and often breeds fancies which sooner or later turn into feelings and resolves. I do not think any such matter of Kitty. I am sure that she was very discreet; and that she mourned heartily and bitterly; and paid very little heed to the next bouquet from Adolphus; and did not triumph so much over Wilhelmina; and tried harder than ever to love her aunt Phœbe; and looked sweetly in her black bonnet; and cried like a child at the grave of poor Truman Bodgers.

Mr. Quid, Senior, bore the family bereavement differently: I say family bereavement, meaning our Fudge bereavement. Mr. Quid, Senior, appeared, however, much interested in the lamentable event.

"Gad!" said Mr. Quid, as he read the announcement of Mr. Bodgers' name in the list of the lost; "the old man is gone at length. Good!"

"It's an ill wind," says the proverb, "that helps nobody." Mr. Quid appeared excited, and walked his little room, ruminating deeply. Not that the demise of Mr. Bodgers brought home to him any thought of his own possible death: he was not the man for such imaginative forays.

He did, however, set about a very earnest examination of certain packages of letters which lay in an odd corner of an old secretary that equipped his chamber. Some few of these he laid aside with much evident glee; now and then rubbing his hands, as he met, perhaps, with some special phrase of endearment; and throwing aside others which, if truth were known, showed even more tenderness of expression, with a shrug of indifference.

After spending a good half day in this sort of mourning over the luckless souls who had gone to the other world under command of Captain ———, Mr. Quid, Senior, dropped a little note to Mr. Quid, Junior, asking him, in an affectionate way, to come and see him quietly on very important affairs.

I shall not undertake to say here what was the result of this interview, save that Mr. Adolphus left in very cheerful spirits, and taking a buggy next morning, drove out to the quiet country village of Newtown.

Nothing was more natural than that a young gentleman of Mr. Quid's brilliant exterior should make a stir in the little village of Newtown; and when it was understood that he was making inquiries in regard to the business and habits of the late Squire, curiosity and expectation were on tip-toe.

Good Mrs. Fleming was not without her conjectures upon the subject: and they were such as might naturally have been expected from a very worthy old lady, who loved her daughter worthily, and was very ignorant of the world. Now Miss Kitty's letters to mamma had not been without their mention of Mr. Adolphus Quid, "an elegant young man, who was very kind, and who visited frequently the Misses Fudge." It is true there was no enumeration of the bouquets which he had sent, or, indeed, of those particular attentions which Kitty (natural-acting girl that she was) chose to keep the record of in her own bosom.

Nevertheless, good old Mrs. Fleming, associating the name in Kitty's letters with the elegant young gentleman who, upon the report of Miss Mehitable Bivins, had just come out to Newtown, had no manner of doubt that, being deeply interested in Kitty, and foreseeing that Kitty would be interested in the settlement of Mr. Bodgers' estate, he had come to Newtown to confer with herself, and to do whatever might be needful and gentlemanly and son-in-law-like under the circumstances.

Acting on this suggestion, Mrs. Fleming arrayed herself in her best bombazine, new-dusted her little parlor, reärranged the books upon the teapoy, and waited the arrival of Mr. Quid.

Mr. Quid, in utter innocence of these motherly arrangements was meantime making inquiries after the legal adviser of the late Squire Bodgers, and presently after called a most extraordinary blush to the cheek of the somewhat lean Mehitable Bivins, by appearing, with his short, ivory-headed cane, at the gate of her father's yard. Mehitable accomplished her Sunday-school toilet in an incredibly short time, but to very little purpose. Mr. Quid desired only to see the Squire on business, and was directed to the office previously described.

The Squire received his city visitor after his usual manner, and relieving himself of a considerable excess of tobacco-juice, he beckoned to a chair opposite.

Mr. QUID. (with the ivory head of his stick at his lips).—"Mr. Bivins, I believe, sir."

SQUIRE.—"That's my name, sir; yes, sir" (raises his spectacles to the top of his head, and pats his wig behind).

QUID.—"I believe, sir, you were legal adviser of Mr. Bodgers?"

"Did some bizness for the Squire; yes, sir" (looking now very narrowly and curiously at the stranger).

"He leaves, I understand, a large property?"

"Well, yes; the Squire was a fore-handed man—well off." (Tobacco-juice among the ashes.)

"He left no direct heirs, I believe?" says Mr. Quid, interrogatively.

Bivins stirs himself slightly in his chair, pats his wig, seems to possess himself of a new idea, and resumes the colloquy, thus:

"Well, no, I guess not; not, as you might say,

in a direct line!" And Mr. Bivins, perhaps at thought of the stately Mehitable, winces at his own joke.

"Ha! ha!" says Mr. Quid; "very good, Mr. Bivins, very good!" Upon the strength of that complimentary sally, and the encouraging twinkle in Mr. Bivins's eye, he goes on to say to Mr. Bivins that he is interested to some extent in the estate, and as he shall have occasion for the professional services of Mr. Bivins, he begs to hand him now a small retaining fee.

Mr. Bivins, in a little wonderment, removes his spectacles from his head and lays them in a careless way upon the top of the bill which Mr. Quid has placed upon the table, as a sort of conditional retainer on his part—of the money.

"And now, Mr. Bivins," says Quid, "will you be kind enough to tell me if Mr. Bodgers made any Will, to your knowledge?"

Mr. Bivins looks carefully at Quid, at his cane, his moustache, pats his wig, considers for a moment, and——is interrupted by a smart but formal rap at his office-door.

The new-comer was no less a personage than Mr. Solomon Fudge. Mr. Bivins knew him at a glance: he dusted his arm-chair with his pocket-handkerchief, and begged the Squire would be seated.

"Perhaps you are engaged, Mr. Bivins?" said Uncle Solomon, in his stately way, at the same time giving a formal nod of recognition to young Quid.

"Oh dear me, not at all, Squire; glad to see you. Sad thing this, about Uncle Truman." And he removes his spectacles from the bill of Mr. Quid, as a kind of tacit relinquishment of claim until he shall have understood the business of the rich Mr. Fudge.

Now Mr. Solomon Fudge has occasionally caught sight of Mr. Quid within his own door, and has heard, moreover, somewhat of his wife's gossip about his attentions to their country-cousin, Kitty. Hence, it occurs to him that he must be making private inquiries about Kitty's chances in the old gentleman's estate; and acting upon this thought, he enters formally upon his business with Mr. Bivins—"presuming that Mr. Quid, from some reports that he has heard in connection with Miss Fleming, is kindly looking after her interest in the estate of his kinsman, Mr. Bodgers."

A new light suddenly illumines the countenance of the cautious Mr. Bivins; and replacing his spectacles upon the bill, he prepares to give the gentlemen just so much of intelligence in respect to Mr. Bodgers and his property, as will pique their curiosity and make his exertions desirable and necessary throughout.

"A large estate, gentlemen, very large; and the Squire consulted me freely; indeed, I may say that I drew up some papers of importance, with reference to his estate, which I guess we shall find at the homestead. What do you say, gentlemen, to calling down at the old place?"

And Mr. Bivins, throwing the bill adroitly into the table-drawer, and turning his key, accompanies Mr. Solomon Fudge and Adolphus Quid to the late home of Truman Bodgers.

They are the two last men in the world that the old gentleman would have chosen for such a visit of inquiry. But in dying, we have to give up not only our characters, but our papers, to the prying eyes and the careless hands of the world: it is well to keep both in order. Death, as Cicero says, in the motto I have put at the beginning of the chapter, is a very bad matter: both for those who have gone through it, and for those who have it to go through.

XVIII.

Wash. Fudge becomes Involved.

"Tell me with whom you live, and I will tell you who you are."
Spanish Proverb.

OUR good cousin Washington is not to be forgotten. We must go back to Paris to find him. He is luxuriating in the way that most very young Americans are apt to luxuriate in the gay capital. It is an odd truth, but confirmed by very much out-of-the-way observation of my own, that if you put a young New-Yorker on the road to the d—l, he will gallop there faster than any youngster of any nation upon the face of the globe. The old adage of the beggar on horseback will occur to the erudite reader; yet it is not *apropos:* a beggar is not often on horseback; but a travelling New-York youngster is rarely pursuing his journey in any other direction than that I have suggested.

Those elegant young gentlemen who introduce the fashions for shirt-collars, small pantaloons, charms, short canes, schottisch, or *matinées*, are not, in a general way, very robust of brain : the atmosphere of Paris is almost uniformly fatal to those who are not robust in that organ. The ladies must explain why it is that such feebleness in our city scions is becoming common. It is my opinion —whatever Mr. Theodore Parker or Miss Abby Folsom may say—that ladies, young and old, are much more accountable for the intellectual and moral habits of our thriving boys, than they are for slavery, or a low tariff. Under the present hop-and-skip aspect of the town society, it is certain that strong-minded ladies content themselves with a side-view, and do *not* take an active part in the entertainment of such young gentlemen as my cousin Wash. Fudge.

In the saloon, however, of the pretty, but middle-aged Countess de Guerlin, Washington found kindness.

Nothing so touches the heart of a stranger in a foreign land as a tender sympathy.

"Oh, *mon petit*," said the charming lady, "I like you so much! and that odious colonel, who has won your money, I detest him; *il est monstre!* But, my dear, it will turn better, I feel ver' sure. Cou-rage, Vashy!"

And the three thousand already mentioned are not all. Indeed, a sight-draft (which my uncle Solomon abominates) is on its way for double the amount. And the little suppers—charming affairs —are more and more frequent; and so are the drives in the pleasant Bois de Boulogne.

Once or twice it does occur, even to the darkened mind of Wash. Fudge, that it might possibly be better to forswear high society, live quietly, and observe a little more attentively what might be worth observing in so extended a tract of country as Europe. Once or twice, I say, this does occur, with a winning fancy of some definite object in life, more than looking on, or dancing, or losing money at "*écarté*;" but it is a shadowy fancy; the straggling remnant of some magazine suggestion, or fragment of a sermon; and has none of the vitality about it which belongs to the graceful speech of the Guerlin.

Moreover, the mamma, Mrs. Phœbe, riding in her claret coach, is she not spending years in just such conquest of brilliant connection as the hopeful Washington has leaped upon at a bound? Is not our lively boy dutifully pursuing the bent of his early impressions? And he slips on in his Guerlin *coupé*, with very much the same quietude of conscience with which the stout woman, my aunt Phœbe, prosecutes her daily drives with the angelic Wilhelmina, amid the delightful scenery of human vanities.

But there are roughnesses even in the soft paths of life; and to anticipate them is almost a conquest. Mrs. Fudge will find it so. Wash. Fudge has found it so.

The draft for five thousand being on its way, Wash., charmed with the Guerlin still, continues to lend the attraction of his presence to the *petits soupers* in the Rue de Helder. The old gentleman in the white moustache is unfailing; and the colonel, the monster, presumes also to be present, and to play unflinchingly at "*écarté*." It is in strong evidence of the disinterestedness of the Countess, that she has never received from Mr. Fudge the amount of her private earnings; she has, indeed, transferred a few of his souvenirs of indebtedness to the gentleman of the white moustache; but Washington feels bold and grateful: he playfully provokes, upon a certain evening, very large bettings with the Countess, and loses. The delicious supper and the excitement of the evening drive the matter out of his mind. Indeed, it might have escaped him wholly, if the colonel had not called upon him a few days after, and urged, in his blandest manner, that he, Wash. Fudge, should cancel that little debt to the Countess.

Washington is surprised. He will call on madame.

"*Pardon;* Madame la Comtesse is engaged to-day."

Mr. Fudge cannot act in the matter without authority from the Countess.

Mr. Fudge may relieve himself of all anxiety, since Madame la Comtesse is the wife of his obedient servant, the Colonel Duprez.

The French are a polite people, as the colonel's manner abundantly proved. He even volunteered an explanation in reply to Washington's expression of distrust.

"I wish to say, Monsieur" (and the colonel tweaks his moustache), "that my wife (*c'est à dire, la Comtesse de Guerlin*) has handed to me these little *billets.* They bear, I think, your name, and a promise to pay, *de vue,* twenty-five hundred francs. *Pas grand chose,* but *les affaires me pressent beaucoup. Je vous attend, Monsieur.*"

"The wife of Colonel Duprez? Impossible!"

"*Vous croyez, Monsieur?*" And the colonel plays with his moustache.

In despair, Mr. Fudge asks if the colonel can wait until to-morrow.

"With the greatest pleasure." And the colonel withdraws, leaving our pleasant hero in a very excited condition. Twenty-five hundred francs are not so very much: but to be so deceived! Surely the Countess can be no party to this imposition. And he is the more confirmed in this opinion by the speedy receipt of a delicate note, in the handwriting of his "distressed Countess."

"She fears that *monstre*, the colonel, has importuned him; has told him—all, perhaps! Oh! the false-heartedness and vexations of the world! Poor, trusting woman! her tears blind her as she writes. Do not, dear Mr. Fudge, be disturbed. *A bientôt.* BEATRICE DE GUERLIN."

And very soon it is that the charming *coupé* stops at the door of Mr. Fudge's hotel, not, as formerly, to command the attendance of our hero; but in the grief of the late disclosure, the Countess worthily abandons her pride, and finds her way in person to the apartment of our excited cousin. Never before had Mr. Fudge taken such pride in the elaborate elegance of his salon; never before had his mirrors reflected such distinguished presence.

And the Countess is bewitchingly dressed: such gloves; such a delicately-fitted boot and waist;

such a coy, half-yielding of the veil! Poor Washington!

"And, *mon cher Vash.*, the colonel has been here?"

"Yes, Madame la Comtesse."

"*Monstre!*—and he has told you"—

"A very queer story, Madame."

"*Ah, mon Dieu! Que je suis malheureuse!*" and the pretty veiled head falls upon the pretty gloved hands, as if tears were being shed.

Washington is sympathetic, and his tones show it.

"*Ah, mon cher!*" says the countess, recovering, and walking up and down in a very excited, but very dramatic manner, "it is too much! too much! He has taken all—all but this poor heart [a dainty glove presses pleadingly upon the heaving bosom], this poor heart—he has not—oh no, no, *mon cher Monsieur!*"

Wash. Fudge *is* sympathetic, and takes her hand—a charming little hand! "Can he do nothing for his dear Countess?"

"She fears not: even her jewels are to be sold."

Wash. Fudge says her jewels shall not be sold.

She does not hear him. "My dear mother's jewels"—

"They shall not be sold: I will save them!" says Wash. excitedly.

"Ah, *quel bon cœur!*" and the Countess looks fondly and gratefully upon poor Wash.

And poor Wash. is failing fast; and the tears gather in the eyes of the Countess; and she hides them: she can hide them only by dropping her head upon the shoulder of our suffering hero.

Now, just as Washington Fudge found himself in this very affecting attitude, the door was suddenly opened (as doors open in melo-dramas), and there appeared the figure of Colonel Duprez!

The Countess shrieked. The colonel looked—iron. Yet he was generous. Washington allowed it; although an aggrieved man, he showed great magnanimity. He led away the Countess in a drooping condition. He turned a last look upon the horrified young Fudge—a look of marble, which was worse, even, than the iron one.

He sent a friend to Mr. Fudge to arrange a meeting for the next day in the Bois de Boulogne.

This did not leave pleasant matter for reflection with our young friend. It is my opinion that New York fashionable education does not cultivate those powers of observation which contemplate gaily a possibility of death, even with broad-swords, or duelling-pistols. And yet, judging from the small-sized limbs belonging to most of the present *habitués* of Broadway, one might suppose they could allow themselves to be shot at from an honorable distance with perfect impunity. Mr. Washington Fudge showed no appreciation of this advantage of person.

I cannot say that he slept soundly. It was a capital thing to boast of, provided he should escape. What a thing to tell down at Bassford's, on his return; or at the New York Club; or to mention incidentally and apologetically at the Spindles's—those elegant people, who had made considerable capital out of a challenge once sent by a third cousin of theirs to Colonel Magloshky! What a thing to hint at, as a trifling occurrence, when dining in company with the tall Captain Gohardy, of Governor's Island!

It has often been a wonder to me what would be precisely the sensations of a man of no very strong nerve, in anticipation of standing up to be shot at. They can hardly be pleasant. There may be a wild sort of satisfaction in shooting at a brutal fellow who has injured you; but for him to have a shot at you, is a different matter. It is a rational admission, so far as there is any rationality in it, that your lives are on a par, and that your own is quite as worthless as his. This, indeed, may well happen; but, so far as my observation goes, it is not currently recognized: most of us possess an instinctive and weakly leaning toward the belief that our own lives are comparatively invaluable. Washington Fudge had long nursed this fancy, in a subdued and quiet way.

It is a very brave thing to fight a duel, but uncomfortable. If a man could be sure of a ball in the right quarter—say the fleshy part of the arm, or of the thigh, or a grazing shot upon one of the ribs; or, indeed, a ball plump through the heart; or no hit at all—it would be well enough. But it is not pleasant to anticipate (especially if one has a slight acquaintance with anatomy) a bullet in the shoulder-joint, occasioning infinite pain, and a crippled limb for life: or a ball in the hip, badly scratching the femoral artery, and bloating up into aneurisms; or in the articulation of the lower jaw, splintering bones of importance; or one in the lungs, producing great wheezing and weak wind for the residue of life; or in the stomach, allowing much gastric juice to escape, and spoiling all thought of dinners for ever.

It is much the same thing with the short-sword; there is no determining in advance what particular spot our antagonist will select for a home-thrust; and under the short-sword excitement, he may be quite as apt to "stamp the vitals" as any other part.

I must confess that I am no duel-theorist. In the place of my cousin Wash. Fudge (which, however, I should cautiously have avoided), I think I should have declined fighting; considering that if my life were worth anything either to Solomon, Mrs. Phœbe, Wilhelmina, or the world in general, or self in particular, it was worth more than that of any such antagonist.

Howbeit, Wash was not strong enough or bold enough to have the world speak ill of him; and although trembling in his shoes at the bare thought of Colonel Duprez and a broad-sword or a pistol, he trembled still more at the thought of the Spindles and the Pinkertons; and he determined to go out.

It was a dull, grey morning which followed upon the arrangement of the meeting, and which was to precede the final catastrophe. At least, our friend Wash. said it was a dull grey morning, in his letter; and such times are apt to be of a dull grey. It was a dull, grey evening, if I remember rightly, that preceded the killing of Macbeth; and it was a dull grey day when Hamlet stabbed the man behind the arras, thinking he was a rat. And it was a dull, grey day when Robinson Crusoe went ashore, and built his cave, and so on; and it was another of the same sort of days when Olivia Primrose ran off with a bad fellow, to wit, young Thornhill. And it must have been, I think (though Thackeray does not mention it), a day of the same color, when Rawdon Crawley was smuggled out of prison, and found Lord Steyne in little Becky Sharpe's parlor, very lover-like and engaging in his manner.

But in the midst of the greyness, the old *Concierge* came up the stairs and delivered a letter from Aunt Phœbe. It is surprising how a letter in a well-known hand, bringing up old-fashioned thoughts and feelings, will often break down the most splendid imaginative flights in the world ; and turn us back by a grasp—not of iron, but of home-knit mittens—from the fancy and ideal world, into a world of almanacs and home-affection ! Even in the most extraordinary epochs of life, when we fancy ourselves giants, or heroes, or saints, a letter from old-time friends, very quaint, very familiar, very full of our old weaknesses, reduces us at a blow to the dull, standard actual ; and convinces us, against our glowing hope and thought, that *we* too are, after all, frail mortals, tied to the poor fabric of every-day life by the same bonds which tied us always ! We never rise to be more than sons, or more than brothers, or more than men. And happy is the calm-thoughted fellow who knows this from the beginning ; and who so orders his designs, that every purpose may help toward the symmetric fulfilment of a destiny, which is only ours by the ordering of Providence ; and which we may qualify by worthy deeds, but never shake from us by a spasm of pride or of anger.

Thus, while Wash. Fudge was about to submit his valuable life to the turn of a short-sword, the mamma was all hopefulness and beatitude ; foreseeing a magnificent triumph for her darling Washington with the Spindles and the Pinkertons. He was casting up his mortal longings and immortal speculations, upon the hinge of two hours' time ; and she, rubicund in her sprawling periods, was enjoying the charming fancy of the elegant young Fudge in Parisian neck-tie and seductive vest-pattern !

" My dear boy," she says, " I hope you are quite well, and have got over the cold in the head you spoke of. It is charming weather in New-York, and old Truman Bodgers is dead ; died aboard the Eclipse, which burnt up two weeks ago, and a great many valuable lives lost, which we regret very much, making true the words of the Psalmist, which I hope you read, that in the middle of life death comes and overtakes us. He has left considerable property, which your father says will be divided between Aunt Fleming and myself, which will make a pretty sum for you by-and-by, being eighty thousand dollars, as Solomon says, in all.

"The Count Salle I spoke to you about, dear boy, is ravished with Wilhe., and I think will propose, though he has not yet. He is a great lion, and the Spindles admire him very much. Papa thinks you are expensive, which I hope you won't be, as it's much better to spend money here than there, because people see it then; unless you wish to marry there, which I don't advise, for fear you will be taken in.

"I told you about little Kitty Fleming, who is pretty. And young Quid, who is distinguished-like, and whom we know, and whom you remember aboard ship, is very attentive to her; only because she is so pretty, we all thought. But papa met him down at Newtown, where he went to look after Truman's property, and thinks he has an eye on the property.

"Now I think of it, Washy, why, since she's pretty, and is to have money, wouldn't it do for you to come home and court her? I don't think Quid has made any proposals as yet; and I am sure with the *éclair* (that's French) of just getting home from Paris, you could make a sensation in society, and so have a very good chance.

"But we wouldn't let this, in case you should come, stand in the way of anything better, and control your affections in any way, my dear boy.

"Try to speak French, and mix as much as you can in genteel French society. I like your acquaintance with the Countess you speak of. She must be a very refined person, and I should like to visit her, which I will do in case I ever go to Paris. Take care of your health, Washy; be careful about your dress; don't spend too much money, now; tie a muffler on when you go in the damp air. And here's hoping you may be an ornament to everybody that knows you.

"From your loving mamma,

"PHŒBE FUDGE."

Washington attempted to leave a few lines for his mother. He went on very well for a sentence or two, when he grew desperate and broke down; exclaiming meantime, much more reverently than he was in the habit of doing, "O Lord!" and shed a few tears.

It was, as I said, a dull, grey morning; and it continued to be dull and grey as Master Fudge pursued his course, thoughtfully, in a hackney-cab, out to the Bois de Boulogne. This wood (for wood 't is) is just outside one of the gates of Paris, and is a scrubby, low forest, where one can find quiet places for duels, or any diversion of that kind.

Never in all his experience of Paris coachmen had Washington found a *cocher* who drove with such spirit and zest. He seemed to advance upon a gallop. The shops flitted dismally by. The fountains, and gardens, and gay equipages, seemed to have lost very much of their charm. And yet Washington was loath to leave them behind him.

Once, in that fast drive, the wheels splashed very near the great gateway of *La Charité;* it was open ; and they were carrying a man upon a litter, whose shoulder had been shattered by a fall. A wounded man upon a litter in the street, with crimson blood dappling the white sheet that half covers him, is at any time an unpleasant sight. But to our friend Wash. it was painful to the last degree.

On and on rattled the furious *cocher.*

"A little slower," said Wash.

And the driver slackened his speed along the quay, where a group of invalid soldiers were lounging on a bench, and reposing their wooden legs.

Washington turned to look upon the river, gliding along placidly enough, bringing down floating weeds and sticks from the laughing country of Bourgogne, which Wash. remembered with a sigh. And over the clanking bridge the hackney-coach rolled on; and under the trees of the Elysian Fields—very Elysian and gay to those of my cousin's taste—and up the long reach of that great avenue, toward the triumphal arch, plunged on the hackney-cab that bore our depressed hero to his first field of battle.

Now, it is my opinion, that the most serious part of the embarrassment which beset the brilliant Wash. Fudge, lay in the fact that the whole drift of his elegant education and his fashionable tutelage bore him as straightly and irresistibly to the duelling-ground as the impetuous *cocher* himself. It was a very awkward way of living up to Mrs. Fudge's mark; or, what would be still more awkward, of dying up to the mark.

A man who puts a reasonable value on his life, has a respectable excuse for taking care of it, and for keeping it, on ordinary, private occasions, out of the reach of musket or pistol-shot. But the man, on the contrary, who lives principally for the attainment of elegant boudoir opinions, has no sort of apology for shirking any demand which the boudoir code of honor may make upon him, whether as the mark for a cool eighteen-pace pistol-shot, or the revolver of an aggrieved husband.

In short, young Wash. was just now paying in the penance of cool perspiration for his extraordinary steps toward high life. And he trembled perceptibly when he landed from his cab upon the spot designated. As yet, no one had appeared upon the ground. Mr. Fudge sauntered about uneasily. The sky was still grey. The sound of the retiring coach had died away; a field-fare or two were twittering in the bushes.

No one approached.

Mr. Fudge looked at his watch, and found it some ten minutes past the hour agreed upon. His spirits revived somewhat. It might be that the colonel had thought better of the matter; at least, there was hope; and he amused himself by calling up old scenes—his elegant mother, the dashing Wilhelmina, the pretty cousin Kitty; all which thoughts, however, were presently dashed by the approaching sound of wheels. The sound grew nearer and nearer. The perspiration gathered upon the brow of Mr. Fudge.

It was not a spot to which a carriage would drive except by appointment. Therefore, when the coachman reined up within a yard or two of Mr. Fudge, he knew there could be no mistake.

A few minutes more, and he felt assured that he would become a hero or a badly hurt man; perhaps both.

At least so it appeared to Washington Fudge;

when the carriage-door opened, and there alighted—the FEMME DE CHAMBRE of the Countess de Guerlin!

This accomplished young lady was the bearer of a note, which ran in the following very incohorent and distressed way:

"Cruel! cruel! *et vous, mon cher!* And can you think that I would suffer your blood to flow under the hands of that *monstre*, whom I will not name? No! no! I know all. I have detained him, but only for a little time, perhaps. Will you fly?

"No; for that would be misery to you: that would be cowardice. I cannot counsel that. Yet the colonel is insatiable, reckless. Misguided, unfortunate woman that I am! O, *cher* Fudge! there is one resource. How dare I name it to one who is the soul of honor?

"Avarice is the bane of my wretched husband's life; yes, avarice! To that I am sacrificed. By feeding that horrid vice, I survive. And you, *cher* Fudge, you too may escape.

"But think not I would sacrifice your honor: *jamais, jamais!* He shall not know. It shall be I will tempt him. Send *me* only so much as will quiet the monster. As you love me and regard my happiness, do not fail. Strange vice! that the miserable sum of three thousand francs should make him wear the charge of cowardice. Yet such is his debased nature.

"Yours, *cher* Fudge, will be the honor ; his the shame.

"Do not fail. *Je vous embrasse mille fois.*

"BEATRICE DE GUERLIN."

It is needless to remark that Washington breathed more freely ; drove to his rooms with the French *femme de chambre ;* revolved the matter ; drew upon my uncle Solomon for a matter of five thousand francs ; and was safe—safe for his dear mother's transports ; safe for the Bodgers legacy.

Life in Paris is very gay for a young man of parts. Subject to ups and downs, to be sure, but gay. On many accounts, it is desirable ; chiefly, however, for those of cool tempers and active brains. I do not think my cousin Washington is possessed of these. I fear he is in the way of difficulty. I have my doubts about the sincerity of this Countess de Guerlin. I may be mistaken.

I hope I am.

END OF VOLUME ONE.

www.ingramcontent.com/pod-product-compliance
Lightning Source LLC
LaVergne TN
LVHW050526100826
845148LV00002B/448

* 9 7 8 1 4 2 5 5 2 0 0 6 9 *